W9-CAY-153

HARVEST OF WAR

Recent Titles by Hilary Green

The Leonora Saga

DAUGHTERS OF WAR *
PASSIONS OF WAR *
HARVEST OF WAR *

WE'LL MEET AGAIN
NEVER SAY GOODBYE
NOW IS THE HOUR
THEY ALSO SERVE
THEATRE OF WAR
THE FINAL ACT

* *available from Severn House*

HARVEST OF WAR

Hilary Green

OAK RIDGE PUBLIC LIBRARY
CIVIC CENTER
OAK RIDGE, TENNESSEE 37830

This first world edition published 2012
in Great Britain and in the USA by
SEVERN HOUSE PUBLISHERS LTD of
9–15 High Street, Sutton, Surrey, England, SM1 1DF.
Trade paperback edition first published
in Great Britain and the USA 2012 by
SEVERN HOUSE PUBLISHERS LTD.

Copyright © 2012 by Hilary Green.

All rights reserved.
The moral right of the author has been asserted.

British Library Cataloguing in Publication Data

Green, Hilary, 1937-
    Harvest of war.
    1. Malham Brown, Leonora (Fictitious character)–Fiction.
    2. World War, 1914-1918–Medical care–Fiction. 3. Love
    stories.
    I. Title
    823.9'2-dc23

ISBN-13: 978-0-7278-8170-0 (cased)
ISBN-13: 978-1-84751-430-1 (trade paper)

Except where actual historical events and characters are being
described for the storyline of this novel, all situations in this
publication are fictitious and any resemblance to living persons
is purely coincidental.

All Severn House titles are printed on acid-free paper.

Severn House Publishers support The Forest Stewardship Council [FSC],
the leading international forest certification organisation. All our titles that
are printed on Greenpeace-approved FSC-certified paper carry the FSC logo.

MIX
Paper from
responsible sources
FSC
www.fsc.org
FSC® C018575

Typeset by Palimpsest Book Production Ltd.,
Falkirk, Stirlingshire, Scotland.
Printed and bound in Great Britain by
MPG Books Ltd., Bodmin, Cornwall.

F
Green

8/2012 011076908 $28.00
Oak Ridge Public Library
Oak Ridge, TN 37830

These books are not romantic fantasies but are based on solid historical fact. They were inspired by the lives of two remarkable women, Mabel St Clair Stobart and Flora Sands. Stobart, who features as a character in this book, was the founder of the Women's Sick and Wounded Convoy. In 1912, she led a group of nurses to care for Bulgarian soldiers during the First Balkan War and returned to help the Serbs during World War I. She gave an account of her experiences in her books *Miracles and Adventures* and *The Flaming Sword in Serbia and Elsewhere*.

Flora Sands was the daughter of a clergyman and an early member of the FANY – the First Aid Nursing Yeomanry. In 1915 she volunteered to go to Serbia with Stobart, was separated from her unit and joined up with a company of Serbian soldiers, with whom she endured the terrible hardships of the retreat through the mountains of Albania. She later returned with them to Salonika and took part in the final advance which ended the war. She was the first woman ever to be accepted as a fighting soldier and ended the war with the rank of sergeant. Though she does not appear as a character in these books, much of the action is derived from her experiences, which are recorded in her own memoir *An English Woman Sergeant in the Serbian Army* and by Alan Burgess in *The Lovely Sergeant*.

Acknowledgements

I am indebted to Lynette Beardwood, archivist for the FANY and fellow of Liverpool John Moores University, for drawing my attention to the stories of Mabel Stobart and Flora Sands and for providing me with invaluable source material about the FANY during World War I.

I should also like to thank my husband for proof reading and my writing group friends Christine and Maureen for their invariably helpful criticisms.

One

The streets of the Greek city of Salonika were crowded with soldiers in the uniforms of different countries. British Tommies rubbed shoulders with French *poilous* and Serbs in their borrowed French uniforms and English boots.

Leonora Malham Brown threaded her way through the crowds in the narrow streets leading down to the harbour. Men stepped back to let her pass and some saluted, but she knew that their respect was due more to the red crosses on her nurse's uniform than to her personally, though some of the Serbs greeted her by name as *Gospodica Leo*. She had earned their respect, and indeed their love, during the terrible privations of the retreat through the mountains of Albania in the winter of 1915 and its aftermath. The long dress and starched apron restricted her stride and she would have been happier in her FANY uniform of riding breeches under a divided skirt, but she had abandoned it for two reasons. The first was the simple fact that the serviceable tweed was just too heavy for Salonika in summer. The second was more complex. It was important for her to give the impression of respectability, for Sasha's sake. He had seen her in many guises, from a ragged urchin to a lady of fashion, but when they had arrived in Salonika a month ago she had quickly become aware that her irregular position as his companion was a source of scandal among the British and French contingents. That would not have mattered to her. She had always been ready to flout convention, but Colonel Count Aleksander Malkovic was more sensitive to criticism. As a Serbian nobleman honour and reputation were of paramount importance to him – and after all, he was married, although to a woman he hardly knew. He had broken his own code by finally giving way to his love for her but she had no wish to publicly embarrass him. Anxious not to be seen as merely a 'camp follower', she had hurried to offer her services at the local Red Cross hospital.

Reaching her destination, Leo paused in the doorway of the restaurant and looked around. The crowded tables had spilled out on to the quayside, the lights from the candles on them reflecting in the water. The sound of laughter and conversation almost drowned the music of the small *bouzouki* band sitting on a low platform in front of the building. It struck her that Salonika was a very different place from the one she remembered first visiting with her friend Victoria. It was still full of foreign troops, but it was no longer a city that had just changed hands after bitter fighting, as it had been back in 1912. The shops and restaurants had opened up again and were doing a roaring trade, and the most fashionable of them all was Floca's, where she now stood.

There was, after all, very little for the soldiers to do. For the last six months they had been bottled up in a small salient that extended from the Adriatic in the west to the River Struma in the east by the Bulgarian army, which was intent on claiming the whole of Macedonia. Unable to break through, the allies had settled for building a wire fence along the frontier, which had earned the area the nickname of 'the birdcage'. Saved from the horrors of the Western Front, the British and French troops had to suffer the indignity of being called 'the gardeners of Salonika'. It was small wonder that they had made the best of their posting. There were football matches and concerts and plays, and every evening when there was no other entertainment on offer they gathered in the bars and cafés to talk, drink and play cards, as tonight. In contrast, the Serbs, after several months on Corfu, were desperate for action and only prevented from staging a new attack by wrangling between the French and their Greek allies.

Leo's gaze searched the crowd until she found Sasha sitting at the edge of the gathering at a table close by the water's edge. He was with two other officers, one British, one French. He saw her and came over.

'You look tired. I expected you earlier. Did they make you work overtime at the hospital?'

Leo had been warmly welcomed by the mixed collection of doctors and nurses of varying nationalities who had volunteered to work for the Red Cross. There were few wounded to care for, but as well as the old enemy, typhus, the visiting troops had fallen victim in large numbers to malaria. Medical resources were stretched to the limits.

'Nobody "made" me,' she said. 'I volunteered.'

'You shouldn't let them put extra work on you,' he responded. 'It isn't fair.'

His tone was slightly petulant and Leo recognized with an inward sigh that now they were lovers he expected her to regard his wishes as paramount. She could not blame him. He had been brought up to believe that women were primarily there to serve their menfolk. Nevertheless, she had no intention of knuckling under completely.

'The regular nurses work just as hard as I do, if not harder. There are so many patients and not enough people to care for them as they should be cared for. Anyway, I'm here now. Shall we join your friends?'

The two officers rose as she approached and the Frenchman exclaimed, 'Ah, mademoiselle, you have come at just the right moment! We are in need of your services as interpreter.'

Leo smiled wryly. It was easy to understand why she was required. Sasha knew only a few words of French and virtually no English; the other two almost certainly knew no Serbian. Until her arrival the conversation must have limped along in German, the only common tongue. Fluent already in French and German, a year nursing Serbian soldiers had given Leo a good command of that language, too.

'I'll do my best,' she said, 'but let me have a glass of wine first.'

It was the perennial topic of conversation: the political impasse with Greece. It was an animated discussion and Leo had to work hard to translate.

'If only King Constantine wasn't such a fool!' Sasha said. 'Does he really imagine that if he stays neutral and the Central Powers win, as he hopes, the Bulgars will meekly take themselves off and leave Macedonia to Greece?'

'It didn't help that General Serrail forced him to demobilize the Greek army,' the British officer put in. 'That has caused a great deal of resentment.'

The Frenchman glared at him. 'Would you rather that they were deployed to assist the Germans? My general was taking a sensible precaution. And that very resentment of which you speak has strengthened the hand of Prime Minister Venizelos.'

'Oh, Venizelos is on our side, all right. But he's only the prime minister. In the end it's the king who has the final word.'

'Don't be too sure.' His French counterpart tapped his nose meaningfully. 'I hear rumours of a planned coup. If Venizelos takes over there will be nothing to stop us opening a new attack.'

'Then I pray God he succeeds, and soon!' Sasha exclaimed. 'If I have to stay cooped up here much longer I shall go out of my mind.'

Leo squeezed his hand under the table. She understood his frustration. When they left Corfu in June he had thought that it was the first move in a campaign that would drive the occupying Bulgars and Austrians out of his homeland. The following weeks of inactivity on top of the long wait in Corfu had driven him to distraction. Her own attitude was very different. For her, every day's delay meant another night they could spend together; a few more precious hours when she did not have to worry about his safety.

Nights like this one. A full moon came up, so that towers and minarets stood out black against the sky, and the tables along the quayside began to empty. Sasha and his two companions ended their inconclusive discussion and finished their wine and they all said goodnight. Sasha had managed to find accommodation for himself and Leo in a small hotel near the port and had booked separate rooms, as a concession to convention. In public they had tried to maintain a decorous distance, until they discovered from various casual remarks that his men had taken their relationship for granted long before they themselves had given in to their mutual attraction. Since then, Leo had hardly ever slept in her own room.

Later, after they had made love and Sasha had fallen asleep,

Leo lay watching him in the moonlight that streamed through the uncurtained window. Asleep, his face was unprotected by his usual expression of proud self-reliance and she could see how the strain of the past months had aged him. There were lines at the corners of his eyes and the hair at his temples was flecked with white. But there was something else as well, a vulnerability that contrasted with her early memories of him. She recalled their first meeting, when he had regarded her with such faintly veiled disdain. 'That insufferable man,' Victoria had called him. Yet even then she had sensed a kindred spirit. 'So damned arrogant,' he had said of his first impression of her, echoing her grandmother's assessment. Well, as she had told him, it was obviously a case of like calling like.

She turned on her back and allowed herself to dream of the future. Sasha had told her that his marriage had never been consummated. It was his engagement to Eudoxie that had stood between them since their first meeting in 1912 but it had never been anything but a marriage of convenience, arranged to heal the long-running vendetta between two families. Eudoxie was fifteen years his junior and suffered from poor health. According to Sasha, his early attempts to 'carry out his duty as a husband' had brought on such violent asthma attacks that he had not persisted, and not long after the wedding he had been recalled to his regiment and war had broken out. He had given instructions for his mother and wife to take refuge in Athens but so far he had not heard from them and had no idea if they had managed to evacuate the country while the borders were still open. But whatever happened, he had promised Leo that when the war was over he would ask for a divorce and they would then be free to marry. She had no doubts about his sincerity. She put her hand to her throat and fingered the locket he had given her when they parted that first time, and which she had worn ever since. He had said that he planned to leave the army once his country was free again and lead the life of a Serbian country gentleman. She imagined the two of them on the estate which she had visited once, on the occasion of his family's 'Slava day'. They would ride out every morning to see how the crops were progressing, pick cherries and plums in season, drink wine produced from their own vines. Maybe they would breed horses. It was a subject that interested them both. The images soothed her and she drifted into sleep.

Leo often remembered with pleasure the rides she had had with Sasha when they were encamped around Adrianople during the war against the Ottomans, and thought sadly of the fate that had befallen their horses on that terrible retreat through the mountains. There was a detachment of *Spahis*, cavalry from French Algeria, stationed in Salonika, and she sometimes watched them exercising their Arab mounts on the beach – beautiful horses whose delicate build belied their capacity for speed and endurance.

One day, Sasha met her at the hospital with the words: 'Come with me. I want to show you something.'

He took her to the cavalry barracks and called to a stable lad to bring out 'the horse'. The boy led out a splendid bright bay and trotted him round the *manege* where the horses were schooled.

'What do you think?' Sasha asked.

Leo narrowed her eyes. 'Good conformation. Nice short back and powerful hocks. Lovely head carriage. Very nice.'

He laughed. 'I'm glad you approve. And, you see, I have taken to heart what an impudent boy once said to me about greys being too conspicuous on the battlefield.'

Leo grinned back at him. It was hard to believe now that once, almost four years ago, he had mistaken her for that youth. 'You've bought him?'

'Yes. After all, I shall need something to carry me when we eventually start the campaign. I am going to call him Plamen.'

'Flame,' Leo translated. 'Yes, very appropriate.'

'Bring out the other one,' Sasha called to the boy.

'Two?' Leo queried.

The boy came back with a chestnut mare with a white star on her brow. 'You told me once your father gave you a horse like this one and she was taken by the army,' Sasha said. 'I thought you might find this an acceptable replacement.'

Leo looked from him to the horse and back again. 'Sasha, she's beautiful! Thank you!'

'She has a name, too. Zvesda – Star.'

Leo climbed over the fence and approached the horse, who stretched her neck and blew through her nostrils at Leo's outstretched hand. The stable boy, smiling, handed her a piece of carrot. The horse took it with delicate lips and Leo slid her hand up the glossy neck and scratched her gently between the ears.

'She likes you,' Sasha said from close behind her.

'And I love her,' Leo replied. 'She's perfect – and you are very kind. I couldn't ask for a better present.'

After that, they rode out together along the beach every day before breakfast. During the day, Sasha drilled his men and conferred with General Bojovic, who now commanded the Serbian army; Leo continued with her duties at the hospital, and at night they slept in each other's arms. It was a time of joy for both of them, but joy for Leo that trembled always on the brink of anguish, knowing that it must be short-lived.

Letters arrived for Leo, redirected from London. There was one from Tom, to whom she had agreed to be engaged in a move which suited them both for different reasons, and a shorter one from her brother, Ralph. Both men were currently fighting on the Western Front. There were two from Victoria, who was in the same area with the FANY. Tom described the beauties of the French countryside as if he was there for a holiday, and Victoria relayed funny anecdotes about incidents in the Calais Convoy, the FANY detachment which had been set up to collect wounded men from the front line and transfer them to hospital. Neither of them spoke of the war, except tangentially, and since all the letters had been written several weeks earlier Leo had no way of knowing if her friends were still alive.

It was over a year since she had left her FANY comrades to join Mabel Stobart's Women's Sick and Wounded Convoy in Serbia, and more than that since she had last seen Tom. Although their engagement had been a matter of convenience for them both, freeing Leo from the oppressive if well-meaning control of her brother Ralph, and providing Tom with camouflage for desires he was afraid to acknowledge, she had developed a genuine affection for him. She found it hard to imagine how a gentle, artistic soul like Tom could survive in the midst of the horrors she had encountered while she was in France. But so much time had passed and so much had happened to her since she left there that her memories had become vague. Tom and Victoria seemed to belong to a different life and she herself was a different person. She wondered what they were doing – and if they had survived until now.

Two

Victoria clung to the steering wheel as a blast rocked the Napier and threatened to turn it over. Ahead, the road was lit up by the flash of explosions and, outlined against the glare, she could just make out the silhouette of the railway station and the adjacent building. Once it had been the veterinary hospital, but now it had been turned over to human use. Above her, the sky was criss-crossed by the beams of searchlights and over the noise of the engine she could hear the roar of aero engines and the scream of descending bombs.

Her companion, a VAD called Monica Dickenson, leaned over and yelled in her ear. 'They're getting a terrible pasting. Do you think we should hold back for a bit?'

'We can't!' Victoria yelled back. 'There are wounded in there to be evacuated.'

She pressed the accelerator and drove the Napier forward. As if some higher power had intervened there was a pause in the bombing and they reached the entrance of the hospital safely. As soon as the ambulance stopped the doors of the building opened and stretcher-parties appeared. Dickenson jumped down and opened the back of the vehicle and four stretchers were hurriedly slid into position.

'Look out!' someone yelled. 'He's coming back. Take cover!'

A man tugged at Victoria's door. 'Quick! Take cover!'

'I can't!' she shouted back. 'I can't leave four wounded men out here. Get in, Dickie! We've got to move!'

Dickenson jumped up beside her and Victoria reversed and turned the Napier to head back towards Calais. As she did so she heard the German plane swoop low overhead and another bomb exploded somewhere behind them. A short distance away she saw a dark shape beside the road.

'That looks like some kind of barn or shed,' she shouted to her companion. 'I'll pull in there and hope he doesn't spot us.'

The open-sided barn offered little in the way of shelter but at least they felt less exposed than on the open road. Victoria turned off the engine and they both climbed into the back of the vehicle, where the four patients lay on their stretchers.

'You girls ought to be in a dugout, not out here like this,' one of the men said.

'Can't leave you all alone, can we?' Victoria replied. 'Cigarette?'

'You're an angel of mercy, and no mistake!' he exclaimed.

One of the patients was only semi-conscious, but the other three willingly accepted cigarettes and they all lit up as the bombs continued to crash around them. Eventually, silence fell and Dickenson climbed down and looked out at the sky.

'I think it's over. It's all quiet.'

'Right!' Victoria scrambled back to the driving seat. 'Let's get out of here while the going's good!'

A few miles away the Second Battalion of the Coldstream Guards was back in billets again after a spell on the front line. This time the officers, including Tom, were housed in a small chateau which had somehow remained undamaged in a fold in the hills. For once, he had a room to himself and was enjoying the unaccustomed luxury of a comfortable bed and the occasional hot bath. Even the mess dinners were no longer as drearily formal as they used to be. Many of the old hands had disappeared: some killed, others transferred to fill the gaps in other units. New men had taken their places, many of them not regular soldiers, and the atmosphere had become much more relaxed and collegiate.

In spite of this temporary improvement in physical conditions, morale was low. After the long months of minor skirmishes they were all weary and bored, and a stream of bad news had done nothing to help. First, word had arrived that the entire British force in Mesopotamia had been obliged to surrender to the Turks; then they read in the papers of the Easter Rising in Dublin and soon after that of the inconclusive battle of Jutland, at which the pride of the British Navy had been humbled by the Germans. No one could see how the present stalemate could be resolved and there was a general feeling that the war would drag on for ever.

The family who owned the chateau had decamped to safer lodgings, but some of the servants, either too old or too young for active service, remained. Among them was a boy in his mid-teens; good-looking after a fashion with full, red lips and thick dark hair which he was constantly pushing back from his brow in what struck Tom as a rather affected manner. His name was Louis and he helped out in the kitchen and generally fetched and carried. He often hung around the officers' quarters, waiting for the chance to run errands, for which he was rewarded with cigarettes and chocolate.

One evening, Tom was in his room, tidying himself before going down to dinner, when there was a knock on the door. Louis stood outside with a glass of Pernod on a tray.

'For you, Lieutenant,' he said.

'No, not me,' Tom responded. 'I didn't ask for it.'

'Yes, for you,' the boy insisted, stepping adroitly round Tom into the room.

'No!' Tom said again. 'I don't even like Pernod. You must have got me mixed up with one of the others.'

Louis put the glass down and gave Tom a lascivious smile. 'You give me cigarettes, yes?'

'No. Why should I give you cigarettes? I didn't send for that drink.'

The boy stepped closer. 'Yes, you give me cigarettes and I . . .' He leaned in and whispered in Tom's ear a suggestion of such extreme obscenity that Tom felt himself grow hot with shame.

He took a sharp step backwards. 'No! You will do no such thing! Get out, and take your foul suggestions with you. I wouldn't dream of indulging in anything so gross.'

Louis's eyes widened mockingly. 'No?'

'No! Now, get out.'

The boy shrugged and moved to the door. As he reached it Tom said sharply, 'And don't go making any such lewd suggestions to any of the other officers, or you might get a hiding. No English gentleman would stoop to anything so low.'

Louis gave him a smile of amused contempt. 'You think?'

He left the room, closing the door softly behind him, and Tom, deeply shaken, grabbed the glass of Pernod and drained it, even though the taste revolted him. He looked at himself in the mirror. Why had the boy approached him? Was there something about his face or his bearing that gave a clue to his awful secret? He thought he had concealed it very well but now he wondered if other people guessed it too, and the thought made him blush again.

Going downstairs he was jolted out of his introspective mood by the sight of a familiar figure standing in the hall. Ralph had been wounded a month earlier and sent home to recuperate. Tom's heart leapt. Ralph had been the most significant presence in his life since his schooldays. They had joined up together and this was the longest time they had been apart since that first day. At Tom's exclamation of delight Ralph swung round and ran to the foot of the stairs.

'Tom! Thank God! You're still OK. Oh, it's good to see you!' He gripped Tom's hand in a fervent clasp and pounded him on the shoulder.

Tom, in a confusion of mingled joy and shame, resisted the urge to embrace him.

'It's good to see you, too. But I'd rather you were still safe in England. How are you? Completely recovered?'

'Fit as a flea and thankful to be back in harness.'

'Really?'

'God, yes! You've no idea how awful it is at home. People constantly asking "what's it like out there?" and "how did you get wounded?" and then the next question is always, "when are you going back?" As if anyone who has been through it wants to talk about it when they get home!'

'I remember,' Tom agreed.

'Oh, I've got news! I had a letter from Leo. She's in Salonika. Have you heard anything?'

'Yes, there was a letter waiting for me when we got back here last week. Thank God she's all right.'

'I wish she'd come home. Can't you write and tell her to get on the first ship?'

'I can write, but it won't do any good. You know that as well as I do.'

The gong sounded for dinner and they went in to join their fellow officers, who were all delighted to see Ralph back. After that there was little time for private conversation.

Three days later, as he left the dining room after dinner, Tom was sent for by the colonel. 'You're not going to like this, old man, but I'm afraid you're being transferred.'

'Transferred? Where to?'

'First Battalion are being moved to the area round Thiepval, near the River Somme. They're very short of officers, so I've had orders to transfer you to them.'

'Why me?' The words came out almost as a bleat.

'Don't ask me.' The CO shrugged. 'God alone knows how the minds of those at HQ work. I'm sorry, old chap, but there it is.'

'When do I go?'

'First thing tomorrow.'

Ralph was not in the drawing room, where the officers habitually assembled after dinner, and someone said they thought he had decided to have an early night. Depressed beyond words, Tom dragged himself upstairs to find him and give him the news. It seemed unjustly cruel that they should be separated when Ralph had only just got back. Reaching the corridor leading to the bedrooms, he was infuriated to see Louis coming out of Ralph's room.

'Damn you!' he exclaimed. 'I told you to keep your filthy ideas to yourself.'

The boy looked at him and sniggered. Then he reached into his pocket and held up a packet of English cigarettes. As Tom stared, he slipped past him, still sniggering, and ran down the stairs. Tom rapped briefly on Ralph's door and walked in.

Ralph was standing in front of the washstand with his trousers round his ankles, washing his genitals. He swung round as Tom entered, water splashing on the carpet.

'Damn it, Tom! Can't a chap have any privacy? What do you want?'

Tom stood and stared at him wordlessly. There was no doubt in his mind about what had been going on, and suddenly the whole idealized edifice he had built up since his adolescence came crashing down. Ralph glared at him for a moment, then reddened and turned away, pulling up his trousers.

'I don't know what you're thinking . . .' His voice wavered uncertainly.

'I know,' Tom said. 'I know what has happened. That boy came to me a few days ago and made the same suggestion.'

Ralph looked round. 'You didn't . . .?'

'No, of course I bloody didn't!'

There was a silence. Then Ralph, his back turned again, muttered, 'Oh, Tom, I'm sorry. I hoped you'd never find out.'

'Find out? What?'

'What a weak, pathetic creature I am. I've tried, God knows I've tried. But there is something in me . . . something that yearns for . . . for . . .'

'For that? For that sordid business with a despicable creature like that boy?'

'No! No, you don't understand. How could you? You're so straight, so honest. We used to snigger about this sort of thing when we were at school and express contempt for those who fancied themselves in love with a pretty boy. Me, louder than anyone! Because I was terrified of what you might guess. I thought it would pass: that one day I would feel differently. But it hasn't. I know that for men like me the only honourable course is abstinence . . . but I don't have the strength.' He turned to Tom, and his face was streaked with tears. 'I need someone, Tom! I need some kind of human contact.'

'But why not come to me?' Tom cried. 'For God's sake, Ralph, you didn't have to suffer like this. If only I had known . . .'

He was about to spill out the story of all the long years of painful concealment but before he could go on Ralph came closer and put his hand on his lips.

'No, Tom. I know you want to help, but there's nothing you can do. You have to understand. All these years you've been the one shining light in my existence. Your honest friendship has kept me sane, made me feel that I'm not completely worthless. If I lost that, I don't know what I should do. I'm more sorry than I can say that you had to find out this way. But if you can find it in your heart to forgive me, to continue to be my friend, that is more important to me than anything else in the world. Can you do that?'

Tom stared at him in dumb misery. 'You know I can. Whatever happens, I would never let you down.'

'I love you, Tom,' Ralph said. 'You are like the brother I never had. Please let me hang on to that.'

Tom swallowed and nodded. He wanted to seize Ralph and crush him in his arms and pour out his true feelings, but with a few words he had put that beyond the reach of possibility for ever. Instead he said, 'They're transferring me to First Battalion. I leave first thing tomorrow.'

Three

Luke Pavel drew the hired buggy to a standstill and pointed ahead with his whip. 'There it is. Welcome to Taupaki Farm.'

Sophie gazed in the direction he was pointing. 'All this? Yours?'

'Well, my Dad's at the moment. Mine one day.'

'Is beautiful!' Sophie was still struggling with English, although Luke had been giving her lessons on the voyage from Cairo.

'Horsey! Horsey! Giddy-up!' cried an excited voice from behind them. Anton had made more rapid progress with the new language than his mother.

Luke turned in his seat and smiled at the little boy. 'Yes,

lots of horses. We'll have to see if we can find you a pony to ride.'

He turned back abruptly and shook the reins to make the horse walk on, aware that his words had contained an assumption that he had no reason to make. That thought segued naturally into the dilemma that had dominated his mind since the ship docked at Wellington. In a few minutes he would have to introduce Sophie to his family – and he did not know what form of words to use. He had written home soon after leaving Cairo and posted the letter when the ship called at Cape Town, but he had ducked the problem of explaining their relationship, simply stating that he was bringing with him a young Macedonian widow and her son, whom he had met by chance during the fighting on Gallipoli and who needed sanctuary and a temporary home. He knew that the reference to her nationality would guarantee her welcome and decided not to muddy the waters by referring to their hasty marriage. That was what he told himself, but he knew that the real reason was that he was so confused in his own mind about the nature of their relationship that he was unwilling to make it concrete in writing. All through the voyage they had maintained a chaste distance. In fact, they had had little choice in the matter as Luke had been accommodated with the rest of the returning troops in a crowded dormitory, while Sophie and Anton had shared a cabin with two other nurses. But during the day they had spent a lot of time together, reminiscing about their earlier experiences at Adrianople and playing with Anton. Luke found himself enjoying both her company and his developing relationship with the little boy more and more as the days passed. They had never spoken of the future. It seemed that they had both tacitly agreed that the duration of the voyage was a time apart from ordinary life, belonging neither to the trauma of the past nor to the uncertainty of the future.

But now the voyage was over and in a moment he would drive up to the door of the farmhouse and be precipitated into the midst of his family. He was longing to see them, and he did not want the homecoming to be clouded by misunderstanding.

There had been no way of letting them know that his ship had docked, but they must have been forewarned somehow because the whole family was assembled on the porch as he drew rein, and for a moment he forgot his dilemma and jumped down to embrace first his mother, then his grandmother and sister, and to exchange a fervent handclasp with his father. His elder sister was married now and living in Taupo, but he was assured she would come to visit the next day. In the middle of these greetings Sophie climbed off the buggy and lifted Anton down, and Luke's grandmother solved the immediate need for introductions by rushing down the porch steps to embrace her with a babble of the Macedonian Serb which was still her primary language. Sophie replied in the same manner and soon she was being welcomed into the house by the rest of the family. No one thought to question why Luke had chosen to bring her to them. She was a fellow refugee from the old country and as such needed no further excuse.

It was not until after a celebration dinner of tender lamb marinated in fragrant spices, combining the abundance of the new country with the traditions of the old one, that the subject was raised. Sophie was putting Anton to bed. Luke's mother and sister were washing the dishes, supervised by his grandmother, and Luke and his father were sitting on the porch with cigars and a bottle of home-made peach schnapps.

Neither of them spoke for a while, until Mr Pavel said, 'You didn't have any trouble getting Sophie through immigration, then?'

Luke put down his glass. He understood that he had been given the cue he needed. 'No. You see, officially, Sophie is my wife.'

'Officially?'

'We were married in Cairo, just before we left. It was the only way the authorities would allow me to bring her on to the ship.'

'Why didn't you mention this earlier?'

'I didn't want . . .' Luke took a long pull at his cigar while he sought for words. 'I didn't want to spoil things, when I had just come home. I was worried that you, or Ma, would be upset.'

'It'll be a shock to your mother, certainly,' his father agreed. 'I don't think it has struck her that you might have had any difficulty bringing Sophie in.'

'But it did occur to you?'

'I have been wondering, yes. But I felt the same as you about spoiling the celebrations.' It was his turn to draw on his cigar and they both smoked in silence for a moment. 'When were you thinking of letting us into the secret?'

'Tomorrow morning, I suppose.'

'Before or after you shared a bedroom?'

'We haven't . . . I'll sleep in my old room.'

'And then? What are your plans for the future?'

'I'm not sure.' Luke hesitated. 'I suppose Sophie will have to find a job somewhere, eventually. She's a qualified nurse, so it shouldn't be a problem.'

His father grunted in assent. 'I guess we can't have too many of them, with all you boys coming back wounded.' He nodded at Luke. 'That leg doesn't seem to give you too much trouble.'

'No. The medics did a pretty good job on it, but it took a while.' He thought back to the endless days on the hospital ship, where men around him died every night and their places were taken by new casualties. He was glad that his parents had not seen the pathetic skeleton to which dysentery and exposure had reduced him. The period of recuperation in Egypt and the long voyage home had allowed time to repair most of the damage. He had put on weight and the blistering sunburn had subsided to a healthy tan. He only limped now when he was tired, but the memories of the horror which was Gallipoli were still fresh. He said, 'I was in a bad way for a while. I probably owe my life to the way Sophie nursed me – in fact, I know I do.'

'You've no idea of making it a real marriage?' his father said. 'You wouldn't be the first man to fall in love with the woman who saved his life.'

Something turned over in the region of Luke's stomach and he took a quick swallow of the schnapps. 'Sophie's a widow, dad. It's only a few months since her husband was shot by the Turks. The question doesn't arise.'

'If you say so,' his father said. After a pause he added: 'I guess it was tough out there.'

Luke hesitated. Should he try to describe the heat, the flies, the insanitary conditions, the suicidal attacks, the incessant sniping? He shrugged. 'Yep, it was tough.'

'Good to have you home, son,' his father said.

'It's good to be here,' Luke responded. He finished his drink and stubbed out his cigar. 'I'm pretty tired, Dad. If you don't mind I think I'll hit the hay.'

'Of course. You get some rest. See you in the morning.'

Sophie had been given the spare room, which happened to be just opposite Luke's, and as he reached his door he saw that hers was slightly open. As he hesitated outside he heard her say softly, 'Luke?'

'Yes.'

He tapped on the door and went in. Anton was asleep in the cot Luke's mother had dragged out of the attic in readiness and Sophie was standing by the open window. The room was lit only by an oil lamp, turned down as low as it would go, and the pale gleam of a waxing moon. The scent of orange blossom from the orchard his grandfather had planted to remind him of home came and went on the breeze. She was wearing a white cotton nightgown, with a shawl round her shoulders, and her dark hair was loose.

He went to stand beside her. 'Can't you sleep?'

'I was waiting for you. I wanted to ask you something.'

'What?'

'You haven't told your parents that we are married. Why not?'

He drew a breath and lifted his shoulders slightly. 'It's difficult. I didn't want to give them too much of a shock. I'll explain it all tomorrow. Well, as a matter of fact, I've just told my father. He sort of guessed.'

'Was he shocked?'

'No, not really. He understood the reason.'

She looked away from him, at the dark shapes of the hills that surrounded the valley. 'I must start looking for a job. It should not be too difficult, I think.'

A chill ran down Luke's spine. 'There's no hurry. You're welcome to stay here as long as you like.'

She shook her head. 'No. I cannot do that. Your parents are very kind, but I cannot depend on your family's charity. I must find a way to support myself and my son, and when I am settled you can divorce me, or have the marriage annulled. It should not be a problem, since we have not . . . I don't know the word.'

'Not consummated the marriage,' Luke finished for her. The chill now seemed to have taken possession of the rest of his body. 'But there is no need to rush things. Take some time to settle in, get used to the place.'

She shook her head. 'No. I am here . . . I don't know how to say it . . .' She reverted to Serbian and he translated.

'Under false pretences. No, you're not, not at all.'

'Yes, I am. As a guest, who is not really just a guest, and as a wife, who is not really a wife.'

Her face was a pale blur surrounded by the dark cloud of her hair and he could not read her expression, but he was suddenly acutely aware of her naked body under the nightgown. In that instant, the confused emotions that had been worrying him for weeks crystallized.

He said, 'Sophie, I know it's too soon to ask this. You are still mourning for Iannis. But . . . one day, perhaps one day soon, would you consider being my wife – in reality?'

Her face lifted towards him. 'This is what you want? What you really want?'

'Yes, it is. But not unless you want it too. You mustn't say yes out of gratitude, or a feeling of being in my debt.'

She reached out and touched his hand and he felt that she was trembling. 'I think . . .' her voice was a husky whisper, 'I think I would like that very much.'

'You mean . . .?'

He did not finish the sentence because she leaned into him and he gathered her into his arms and kissed her. Her lips were soft and responsive and he felt her body straining against his own. After a few minutes he lifted her up and carried her silently across the passage to his own bed.

Luke woke to a sense of completeness, as if he had come to the end of an episode in his life. Now, at last, he could put the horrors of Gallipoli behind him and begin anew. He looked at Sophie, asleep beside him with her dark hair spread over the pillow. They had made love almost silently, partly because they were both aware of the rest of the family still awake and moving around the house, but also because their passion had an almost dreamlike intensity, suffused with a great tenderness. It was completely different from his memory of his abortive encounter with Victoria, back in Lozengrad, and this added to his sense of embarking on something new. In a matter of a few hours his life had turned a corner and suddenly he found himself with a wife . . . and a son. He was not sure whether he would ever be able to think of Anton as really his, but he resolved at that instant that if he had any reservations the little boy should never be aware of them.

There was one shadow over his contentment. His leg was healing, and he was still in the army. Sooner or later he would have to appear before a medical board and, if he was deemed fit, he would be returned to the front. He told himself that perhaps the war would be over before that time came, but he could not place much confidence in the possibility.

From across the hall Anton began to cry and call for his mother, and Sophie rolled out of bed almost before she was awake. Before Luke could speak she had struggled into her nightgown and was at the door and face-to-face with his mother, who had also heard the child's cries. For a second the two women stared at each other and then, with a muttered apology, Sophie dodged past and went into her own room. Luke had pulled on his pyjama trousers by this time and hurried over to his mother.

Mrs Pavel looked past him at the rumpled bed and then round at the open door of Sophie's room. 'Ah,' she said, and the single sound incorporated disapproval and a fatalistic accept-ance of the situation, as she saw it.

Luke put his arm round her, grinning. 'It's all right, Ma. We're married.'

'You're what?'

'We got married in Cairo, because it was the only way I

could bring Sophie on the ship. It was supposed to be just a marriage of convenience, but last night we decided it would be more convenient to be married properly – if you see what I mean.'

'Well, why didn't you say?' Sophie came out of the bedroom with Anton in her arms and Mrs Pavel turned to her. 'If I'd known yesterday that you were part of the family, I'd have given you a proper family welcome. Come here, my dear, and let me do it now.' She put her arms round Sophie and the child and kissed them both. 'Welcome to Taupaki!'

Four

In the valley of the Somme the fields sloping down to the river were brilliant with poppies and cornflowers and loud with the hum of insects. For Tom, lying on his back among the long grass, the sound was almost sufficient to drown the noise of the guns bombarding Verdun, a few miles away. Everyone knew that there a bitter struggle was under way, as the Germans threw the whole might of their army against the French defenders; but here, apart from the routine exchange of gunfire which occurred at a recognized hour every morning and evening, the battle front was quiet. It was an uneasy quiet, though – everyone knew that a 'big push' was being planned. It was just a question of when.

So far there had been little fighting in this area. The British and German lines faced each other across the space of no-man's-land and from time to time patrols went out at night to check for sapper activity, but there were no organized attacks; in fact, the opposing sides had developed an almost comradely attitude. Rumour had it that the officers of one battalion had been horrified to discover, upon relieving another unit, that the German officers from the opposing sector were in the habit of popping over every evening after dinner for a game of bridge.

But behind the lines the peaceful countryside was

being torn apart by new roads and railway lines, and along those routes rattled and trundled huge numbers of guns – mortars, howitzers and field guns of varying calibre. Telephone wires were sunk into the ground and ammunition dumps set up, new trenches were dug and it was obvious to any observer that preparations were being made for the greatest battle yet.

For Tom, the transfer to First Battalion, which had come as such a shock, had proved a blessing. After their last encounter he did not know how he could have faced normal daily contact with Ralph. Here, among strangers, he had time to reflect. Not to recover – he recognized that he had been given a wound that would never heal – but at least to come to terms with the shattering of his dream. He had never expected to be able to declare his true feelings to Ralph, but to discover that the possibility had existed and then to have it snatched away was too cruel to bear.

Art and distance were his saviours. In the breathless pause before the new offensive there was little for him to do beyond the basic routine of inspections and drills, so he had time to explore the countryside. In the gardens of abandoned cottages, roses grew unpruned and bushes of gooseberries and blackcurrants, heavy with fruit, offered nourishment to both eye and tongue. Twice he borrowed a bicycle and rode into Amiens, where he stood in awe in the cathedral. Soon, his sketch book was full of images of beauty instead of pictures of horror and devastation.

One evening the commanding officer of his company, Captain Barton, said casually, 'You a fisherman, Tom?'

'What sort of fishing did you have in mind?' Tom responded cautiously.

'Fly, of course. You didn't think I meant working on a trawler, did you?'

'Well, yes, I have fished, but not for a long time.' It had been one of the few country pursuits he had enjoyed as a boy, largely because it gave him an excuse to disappear from the house and spend hours sitting by a stream with a rod nearby and a sketch book on his knee.

'I was thinking, there must be trout in this river – what's it called?'

'The Ancre.'

'That's it. You're off duty tomorrow, aren't you? Why don't you take a horse and have a ride upstream and see if you can spot any likely-looking places where we might cast a fly. Then, next chance we get, we can go out and try our luck.'

'I don't have a rod with me,' Tom pointed out.

'That's no problem. I have a spare you can borrow. What about it?'

'Why not? It sounds a good idea.'

For one idyllic day Tom was almost able to forget the war. He took a horse from the lines, one that he had ridden before and knew to be quiet and easy to handle, and jogged gently along the river bank until he came almost to the source. Then he rode slowly back, stopping frequently to sketch likely spots for catching the trout he could see in the clear water, lazily holding their places against the current. Barton was delighted with his efforts, and two days later they rode out again, accompanied by an orderly, and returned with enough gleaming brown trout to make a welcome variation to the diet in the mess.

Very soon they had a rude reminder that they were at war. It was not unusual to wake in the morning to find that some enterprising German patrol had left a half-joking notice fixed to a post in no-man's-land, taunting the opposing forces. One day, the words on the sign had a much stronger impact, in spite of the erratic English. *The English Ministre of War and the General Kommandre Lord Kitchener is on the trip to Russia with all his officers drowned in the east sea by a German submarine.*

'Is it true, do you think?' Tom asked his CO.

'God knows! It'll be a bad blow to morale if it is.'

Within the next twenty-four hours they had confirmation. Kitchener, the inspiring figure who had persuaded thousands of young men to join up, was dead.

A few days later Barton came back from a conference with his senior officers.

'Well, men, this is it. The Big Push starts in four days. There will be a massive three-day bombardment before that. You've all seen the build-up of firepower. Once our artillery has finished with them there won't be a German left alive. We

should be able to walk through the gaps in the wire and into
their trenches without firing a shot.'

One of Tom's fellow subalterns turned to him and muttered,
'Why does that remark not fill me with confidence?'

Tom stood on the fire step with his whistle in his mouth
and his eyes on his watch. His head was pounding and he
felt sick with fear and lack of sleep. The attack had been
put off for two days because of bad weather, so for five days
the artillery had pounded the German trenches with a relent-
less rain of shells. The noise had been incessant. The smaller
shells whistled and howled. The big ones sounded like an
express train passing overhead. The explosions blended into
one continuous roar. It was hard to see, indeed, how anything
could have lived through it, and there had been no answering
fire from the German lines. Around him some of the men
had been joking, laying bets on how far forward they would
be by the end of the day, but now a tense silence had fallen.
Tom had not joined in the optimistic predictions. Whether
they were correct or not, he had a premonition that he
would not survive the day. The thought did not distress him.
At least it would put an end to the pain in his head.

Suddenly the guns fell silent and in the breathless pause that
followed, incredibly, Tom heard a lark singing. All along the
line there were smaller explosions as smoke bombs were let
off, and immediately the ground between the lines was covered
in a dense pall. It struck Tom that if any Germans were still
alive they would know at once that the attack was about to
commence. All along the trench whistles blew. Tom blew his
and drew his revolver.

'Come on, lads!'

He scrambled up the ladder propped against the side of the
trench and stood in the open. To both sides of him men were
forming up in line, in perfect skirmishing order. Their orders
were to advance at a steady walking pace and in an unreal
silence they plodded forward, each man weighed down by
sixty-five pounds of equipment and ammunition, skirting shell-
holes where possible, or splashing through them. As they came
closer to the German wire there was still no answering fire

and Tom began to believe that perhaps this time what they had been told was true. He searched ahead for the gaps in the wire which the barrage was supposed to have created and could see none. He was just beginning to wonder why when the machine guns in the German positions opened up. Along the line to his right men began to fall like dominoes, as if it was part of some gymnastic exercise. It took him a split second to understand why, then he threw himself to the ground just as the traversing fire reached him.

After a few seconds he heard shouting behind him and realized that the second wave had left the trenches and were advancing. He stood up, gripped by a strange fatalistic calm, and began to move forward. On either side, other men were scrambling to their feet. He waved to them and shouted, 'Come on, lads!' In a shell-hole to his right a man was crouched, as if doing up his boot laces. 'Get up!' Tom yelled. 'Come on, up!' He leaned down and shook his shoulder and the man keeled over on to his side. Tom saw that bullets had carved a line across his waist, almost cutting him in half. The man's intestines were bulging out and even in death he was clasping them with both hands as if trying to shove them back. Tom straightened up and struggled forward.

There were others with him now, no longer a straight disciplined line but a rabble of desperate men. He saw more of them fall on either side of him, and the bodies of the dead and wounded barred his way. He jumped over some, trampled on others, and found himself at a gap in the wire. Ahead was a trench. He pulled a Mills bomb from his belt and lobbed it in, then ducked until the explosion was over. Jumping into the trench he saw five Germans. Four were dead. The fifth was reaching for his rifle. Tom raised his revolver and shot him in the head.

There was a slither of stones behind him and a man from his platoon dropped into the trench, quickly followed by two others.

'What now, sir?' one asked breathlessly.

'We must hold this section of trench until the reserves come through,' Tom said. 'Try to find something to barricade either end. And collect all the grenades you can find.'

They could hear German voices approaching as reinforcements arrived. Tom took a grenade from the body of one of the Germans and lobbed it round the traverse at the end of the trench. There was a scream and the advance seemed to pause. The men with him dragged everything they could find, including the dead bodies, to each end of the section and piled them up, but it was not long before a grenade landed close to one of them, the fuse still fizzing. Without hesitation, the man picked it up and hurled it back and they heard it explode on the far side of the barricade.

How long they held out Tom was never sure. They threw every grenade they could find, more than once returning those that were thrown at them, and each one gave them a brief respite, but it seemed that at any moment the enemy must break through and overwhelm them. Then, at last, the attacks ceased, there was a sound of English voices and a second lieutenant in the Somersets led a small party into their section of the trench.

'Bloody good show!' he exclaimed. 'You can fall back now. There's a German sap just to your left. If you follow that it'll take you back nearly to our lines.'

Numb and almost too weary to move, Tom led his small contingent along the sap, finally fell into his own front-line trench and lost consciousness.

He came round on a stretcher in the forward dressing station. An orderly was bending over him. 'Am I wounded?' he asked.

'Nasty cut on the head, that's all,' the man said. 'We thought it was worse to begin with. You were so covered in blood we didn't hardly know where to start looking. Seems like most of it wasn't yours.'

As he lay waiting for the wound to be stitched Tom tried to come to terms with what he remembered of the last hours. It was hard to focus his thoughts, but he could not escape a feeling that he had crossed some kind of threshold . . . that he would never be the man he was a day earlier. He remembered that he had shot a man, quite deliberately, and had felt no compunction. In the struggle for survival his most primitive, atavistic instincts had taken over and even now he felt no regret, but rather a vague sense of triumph. They had taken the trench and held it, against all opposition. He wondered how far the advance had gone beyond that point.

When his wound had been treated he was free to return to his unit – if he could locate it. The trenches were a milling chaos of wounded men and stretcher-bearers and it took Tom some time to find an officer.

'God knows!' was the answer to his question. 'It's a nightmare out there. You'll be lucky to find any of them alive.'

Tom discovered what was left of his company occupying a German dugout just behind the first line of trenches. Barton was there, one arm in an improvised sling, his head drooping in exhaustion.

He looked up as Tom clattered down the stairs. 'Tom? Thank God! We'd given you up for dead.'

'What are we doing here?' Tom asked. 'I thought we'd be further forward than this.'

The captain gave a brief, bitter laugh. 'You went over the top with the first wave, didn't you? You saw what happened.'

For the first time Tom remembered the domino collapse of the men on either side of him. 'I don't understand. What went wrong?'

'Look around you. How deep is this dugout? Thirty feet? Nothing short of a direct hit by a high-explosive shell would affect anyone in here. The Jerries just sat out our bombardment in their cosy little bolt-holes and then, as soon as the shelling stopped, all they had to do was run up the stairs and man the machine guns.'

'How many have we lost?' Tom sank down on a packing case.

'God alone knows. Hundreds, thousands. And all for a few forward trenches. Fritz will counter-attack as soon as he can bring up reserves and we'll be lucky to hold on to what we've gained. What a bloody shambles!'

Five

At some point in the days following the first assault at Thiepval Tom decided that alive or dead it made no difference. He was already in hell. Again and again they were ordered to attack, and again and again he led his men towards the enemy guns. Sometimes the advance ended with hand-to-hand fighting in the German trenches; sometimes it petered out in the craters of no-man's-land. Sometimes they gained their objective: the crest of a small hill, or a copse of trees reduced to skeletons by the bombardment. Sometimes they were able to hold it; more often they were driven back by a determined counter-attack. Death became commonplace. Replacements for men lost were sent up and died before he even had time to learn their names. He trampled over bodies as if they were fallen branches. Often he had no food for days on end. He took rations from corpses, drank from dead men's water bottles. Yet still he survived. He came to the conclusion that this was his punishment. Not for him the peace of oblivion; he must live on as punishment for what he had become, what he had allowed the war to make him.

One day, he heard that the Second Battalion had been withdrawn from Ypres and sent to reinforce the troops on the Somme. That meant that Ralph was somewhere in the vicinity, if he was still alive. But he had no chance to enquire. Social interaction had been reduced to the barest necessities. Then, at last, they received the order to retire and regroup. For the first time, all three battalions of the Coldstream Guards were to attack in line. The objective was the village of Les Boeufs and the news that the whole regiment was to be together seemed to cheer the troops considerably.

'Now we'll show them!' Tom heard. 'Fritz won't know what hit him!'

He could not share their optimism.

The attack began at 8.30 a.m. and once again Tom forced

his limbs to carry him out of the trench and forward up the slope of the long hill ahead, shouting to his men to follow. Enfilading fire from machine guns on the crest was kicking up the dust to either side of him but he ignored it. Suddenly a new sound, audible above the chatter of the guns and the crash of exploding shells, caught his attention: a grinding, throbbing roar that came from somewhere to his left, and with it a wave of cheering. Looking round, he was stopped in his tracks by an extraordinary apparition. A huge machine, a steel leviathan that moved forward not on wheels but on some kind of moving belt, was advancing towards him, crushing beneath it every obstacle in its way. From the top of it a gun spat fire towards the enemy trenches and following behind it were a throng of cheering soldiers. The enemy gunners had seen it too and for a moment all firing ceased. The machine ground forwards, smashing through the enemy wire as if it was made of gossamer and rolling unimpeded over the first trench. Tom saw German soldiers scrambling out of its path and fleeing. The British men rushed forward in pursuit and Tom ran with them. But suddenly a spurt of black smoke issued from the rear of the machine and the engine choked into silence, leaving it tilted to one side like a beetle left helpless on its back. The advance faltered and came to a standstill and the enemy guns opened up again.

A shell exploded at the feet of the man next to Tom, leaving a smouldering crater and showering Tom with earth and fragments of human flesh. He heard the whistle of a second shell approaching and instinctively flung himself sideways into the still smoking hole. He lay for a while, panting and listening to the sounds of the battle around him. He could tell from experience by the noise whether the advance was continuing or whether it had stalled. This one, like so many before, had stalled. The survivors would cower in their shell-holes until dark and then try to crawl back to their own lines. He knew he should get up and try to rally them but he was exhausted and sick of the whole business. Then, a little way off, he heard the unmistakable notes of a hunting horn, followed by a ragged cheer. He raised his head cautiously. A figure he recognized as Colonel Campbell, the commander of the Third

Battalion, was running forward, hunting horn in one hand, revolver in the other, and his men were racing after him. Tom scrambled out of the shell-hole and joined them. In a wave they swept towards the enemy trenches. To his amazement Tom found his section empty. He drew a Mills bomb from his belt and threw it round the traverse wall, then went in after it. A figure appeared in front of him. He fired and the man fell. Others from Tom's own company were behind him now and he led them along the communications trench towards the second line.

Time and distance became a blur. He ran and fired, reloaded and ran on, hearing the shouts and cheers of men on either side and, when they began to falter, another call on the horn. As dusk began to fall they found themselves entering the ruins of the village of Les Boeufs. In what remained of the village square Colonel Campbell called them to a halt.

'We'll dig in here for the night, men. We're far ahead of the rest, so we'll hold this position until the reinforcements come up.'

Suddenly Tom felt that his legs would not hold him up any longer. He sank down with his back against a broken wall and closed his eyes.

A voice nearby forced him to open them again. 'Cup of char, sir?'

A soldier was crouching in front of him with a steaming mess tin. He took it and thanked the man.

'Something to eat, sir? It's only hard tack, I'm afraid.'

Tom shook his head. The thought of food turned his stomach. He sipped the tea gratefully, then closed his eyes again and slipped into a sleep that was like a coma. When consciousness returned he was stiff and shivering in the damp chill of dawn and the village was astir with the sound of tramping feet and new voices. An orderly with a Red Cross arm band approached him.

'Better let me have a look at that wound, sir.'

'Wound? I'm not wounded,' Tom said.

'Don't know about that, sir. Look at your tunic.'

Tom looked down. His tunic was ripped across the shoulder and stained with blood, and when he tried to lift his hand a stab of pain went through him. The orderly efficiently cut away the remaining material, exposing a deep gash from which blood was oozing.

'That's going to need proper attention, sir,' the orderly said. 'It needs stitching, and the bullet could still be in there. I'll tell my CO.'

He bandaged the wound tightly and a few moments later a captain, whose name Tom did not recall, came over to him.

'Can you get yourself back to the dressing station? We're taking over here so all you chaps are being withdrawn. Bloody good show, incidentally! Do you think you can manage?'

'I expect so.' Tom hauled himself to his feet. A steady stream of men was heading back down the hill towards the British lines, but it was a trickle compared to the flood that had swept the Germans aside. Bodies littered the ground and they had to pick their way over them. The Coldstreamers had paid a heavy price for their victory.

Tom was never quite sure how he ended up at the dressing station. At some point he must have passed out, because he came round on a stretcher with a doctor bending over him. The doctor took a cursory glance at the wound and said to someone Tom could not see, 'Not serious. He can wait.'

He waited, the pain in his shoulder growing more insistent, until it seemed to consume his whole torso. Finally the doctor came back, probed the wound and pronounced it clear. He gave Tom a morphine injection, stitched the wound and put his arm in a sling.

'Right,' he said. 'I can't see that that wound warrants sending you back home. The truth is, there are hundreds of men in a worse situation than you are. But you've lost a lot of blood so you need to take it easy. I'm going to send you back to Battalion HQ for them to decide what to do with you. If you're up to it, there's a car leaving in a couple of minutes that will take you.'

Battalion HQ was in a ruined farmhouse a mile or so behind the lines. Tom reported to a corporal sitting at a table in what had once been the kitchen and was asked to wait. He sat in a kind of stupor, wondering vaguely how long it would be before someone offered him something to eat or drink. His throat was so parched he could barely speak.

The corporal returned. 'Major Malham Brown asks you to come this way, sir.'

Ralph was sitting behind another table, spread with maps. He got up as Tom was announced and hobbled forward. Tom registered that his left foot was in a cast and he supported himself with a stick.

Ralph grasped Tom by his good shoulder. 'Tom! Dear God, what have you been doing with yourself? You look terrible. But you're alive, that's all that matters! I've been worried out of my mind.' His voice broke. 'I'm just so glad to see you!'

Suddenly Tom's legs buckled under him and he felt himself caught in Ralph's arms. He pressed his face into Ralph's shoulder and began to weep: silent, shuddering sobs that shook his body and tears that scalded his eyes and soaked into Ralph's tunic.

Above his head he heard Ralph murmuring, 'What have they done to you? It shouldn't happen like this. Not to you! I won't have it. It's got to be stopped.'

At length the paroxysms of weeping exhausted themselves and Ralph led him to the side of the room, where a camp bed had been set up. They sat side by side, Ralph's arm still round Tom's shoulders.

'Look at you!' he murmured. 'You're a walking skeleton. When did you last have a square meal, or a decent night's rest – or a bath?'

Tom shook his head. 'God knows. I've been living like an animal for weeks. What about you? What happened to your leg?'

'Broken ankle. I tripped over some barbed wire and fell into a trench. Bloody stupid! I've been stuck back here at HQ while you chaps are out there doing the business. I look at you, Tom, and I'm ashamed.'

'It's not your fault,' Tom muttered.

'Where are you wounded? Is it your arm?'

'No, my shoulder. It's just a flesh wound. But apparently I've lost a lot of blood.'

'Right!' Ralph straightened up. 'You are going to have the

best that this godforsaken place can provide. You are going to have a meal and a bath and sleep in a proper bed and then you are going on sick leave.'

'The doc said it wasn't bad enough to warrant being sent home.'

'I don't care what he said. I'll make out the necessary pass. Now, what do you want first?'

'Please can I have a drink of water?' Tom croaked.

'Water? Of course! What have I been thinking of? Here.'

There was a jug on the desk. Ralph poured water into a mug and placed it in Tom's good hand. His throat was almost too dry to swallow but he allowed the water to trickle into his throat and almost wept again with sheer relief. Ralph was shouting for his orderly and when the man appeared told him to see to it that Tom was given the best meal the kitchen could produce.

Next morning, still weak but in control of himself after a long sleep, Tom was eating breakfast when Ralph came in and sat opposite him.

'Now, about this leave. Where do you want to go?'

Tom struggled to adjust his thoughts. 'I don't want to go home. I think I'd like to go to Paris. Is that possible?'

'Certainly. I'll make out the paperwork.'

Within the hour Tom was provided with a new uniform and handed a warrant that allowed him to travel to Paris for two weeks' leave. Ralph even arranged for a car to take him to the station and came to see him off.

'Don't overdo it now,' he counselled. 'No riotous nights with girls from the Folies Bergère.'

Tom looked at him. 'That's not my style – and you know it.'

For a moment their eyes held, then Ralph did an extra-ordinary thing. He leaned into the car and kissed Tom on the cheek.

'Off you go! Have a good leave – and don't worry about the future. You're too valuable to be wasted.'

In Salonika the days passed too slowly for both Leo and Sasha, but for opposite reasons. Sasha was bored and frustrated with the lack of agreement over tactics. Leo longed for the summer to end so that the time for campaigning would be over for another year. They would have the whole winter together. But even as she thought of that she felt a tremor of dread. She was not sure how Sasha would cope with being confined to Salonika for all that time and she feared he would embark on some rash exploit without waiting for his allies.

One evening Sasha came quickly into their room at the hotel in Salonika and Leo felt her heart give a jolt.

'It's come!' he said. 'Serrail has finally decided to attack. There are rumours that Romania is about to declare for the allies and they want a diversionary assault here to draw away German forces that might otherwise be deployed against the Romanians.'

'When?' Leo asked, almost unable to breathe.

'In five days, on August the fourteenth.'

Five days! Now that the time was almost upon them, Leo cast about desperately for some way to delay their separation. At the hospital she waylaid the chief medical officer on his rounds.

'I suppose you have heard that there is to be a new campaign?'

'Of course.'

'I assume you will be sending out a field hospital to care for the wounded.'

'Are you trying to tell me my job?'

'No, of course not. I just want to volunteer to go with them. I have had experience of working in the field – and I speak Serbian and Bulgarian.'

'Very well. I'll bear that in mind.'

'Then I can go?'

'I'll let you know when I've made my decision.'

Leo was left to chew her nails until news came that changed all the plans that had been drawn up. The Bulgarians, presumably warned in advance by friends in Greece, launched a pre-emptive attack and Sasha and his men, along with their British and French allies, were caught up in a desperate defensive action. The planned advance was put off until September the twelfth.

'Isn't that too late to start a new campaign?' Leo asked when Sasha told her. 'Winter comes early in the mountains. You don't want to be caught up in the sort of conditions we suffered last year.'

'If we don't go then we shall have to wait until spring,' he said. 'And who knows what might have happened? We have to take our chance. With any luck we shall be through the mountains before the bad weather comes.'

As September the twelfth loomed closer it occurred to Leo for the first time that she might be pregnant. Her periods had stopped after the privations of the winter retreat and, although they had restarted while they were on Corfu they had been irregular, so she had not paid much attention to when the next one was due. But one morning she woke feeling queasy and all day she was aware of a tightness in her breasts. Thinking back, she realized that she had not had a period since the night when she had first slept with Sasha. He had taken precautions since then but in that first passionate encounter neither of them had thought of the risk. She wondered whether to tell him of her suspicions but immediately decided against it. If he thought she was carrying his child it would only add to his burdens. He would have enough to contend with, without worrying about her. He would probably forbid her to join the field ambulance, assuming she had the opportunity. Worse still, he might insist on her going back to England, where she could be sure of better medical attention. She had no intention of obeying such an order, but she did not want to quarrel just as they were about to part. She decided to say nothing until winter brought an end to the fighting, at least for the time being.

On the night of the eleventh they made love with an aching tenderness and in the morning she watched him mount Flame and said goodbye to him with all the courage and optimism she could muster. Then she reported for duty and was told to make ready to leave with the field hospital the following day.

In Wellington, the capital of New Zealand, Luke attended a medical board and was passed fit for active service.

'Congratulations!' the chubby doctor in charge said to him. 'I'll bet you're itching to get back to your mates and give the Boches what for.'

Luke restrained an impulse to punch his self-satisfied face. 'Not if it's going to be anything like the last shambles,' he said bitterly. 'Besides, I'd been hoping for a few months longer. My wife's pregnant. I'd like to have been around for the birth.'

Six

Tom spent the first two days of his leave sitting in Notre Dame, absorbing the atmosphere of indestructible peace. From time to time he got up and wandered round, gazing at the windows, the statues, the works of art of all kinds that adorned the cathedral, but most of the time he sat and let his mind go blank. On the third day, he got out his sketch book and began to draw, filling the pages with details of soaring columns and intricate carvings. When he felt stronger, he made his way to the Louvre and stood for a long time in front of the Winged Victory, contemplating the product of another warrior society and wondering if anything of beauty could result from the brutal conflict he had just left behind him. A few days later he summoned the energy to climb up to Montmartre and stroll through the narrow streets where every shop front, it seemed, exhibited the work of another painter. It reminded him of his first visit, four years earlier, in pursuit of Leo; a visit which had opened his eyes to so many possibilities.

He did not think about what awaited him at the end of his leave. He had learned to live in the moment, whether of joy or terror. But from time to time he did allow himself to contemplate Ralph's final, enigmatic words: 'Don't worry about the future. You're too valuable to be wasted.' Too valuable to whom? To the world in general? That was patently nonsense. To his country? Only in a very marginal sense. To Ralph himself, then? Perhaps. He held the thought close, like a child clinging to a favourite toy.

At the end of two weeks, stronger in body from eating well, as it was still possible to do in Paris in spite of the war, and sleeping as long as he needed to, he took the train back to Amiens and from there managed to get a lift back to Battalion HQ. He headed straight for the room where he had found Ralph on the previous occasion, but it was occupied by a stranger.

'I'm looking for Malham Brown,' he explained.

'Not here, I'm afraid,' was the answer. 'He went back to his company two days ago.'

'Back to the trenches?'

'Yes. They are somewhere near Morval, I believe.'

'Thanks.' Tom turned away. It had not occurred to him that Ralph might have gone back to active duty and the disappointment left him feeling chilled and empty. He made his way to the office of the adjutant and reported.

'Ah, Devenish! I've got news for you. You're being posted.'

'Posted? Where to?'

'They want you back at GHQ.'

'Why?'

'No idea. No doubt you'll find out when you get there. I'll make out the necessary travel documents for you. You can leave tomorrow.'

The British Fourth Army had taken over as its headquarters the Chateau de Querrieu, an elegant rose-coloured building lying in the gentle valley of the River Hallue. When Tom reported he was told that none other than the C-in-C, General Rawlinson, wanted to see him. He found the general with several junior officers in the ornate salon, which had been converted to serve as operations centre for the army, its walls hung with maps and much of the furniture shrouded in dust sheets. When Tom saluted and introduced himself Rawlinson dismissed the others with a courteous, 'Thank you, gentlemen,' and led him over to a table by one of the windows. There, among the piles of papers and diagrams, Tom was astonished to see one of his own sketch books. He recognized it as one he had left behind when he was transferred to the First Battalion, after that disastrous encounter with Ralph. Ralph must have found it, he guessed, but how it had come into the general's possession he could not imagine.

'So, you're Devenish,' Rawlinson said. 'And I gather this is your work.'

'Yes, sir.' Tom wondered if he was about to be reprimanded for wasting his time when he should have been devoting himself to military matters.

'You have a remarkable talent,' the general went on. 'I have been told that on several occasions your sketches of the battle-field have been of considerable use to your commanding officers.'

'I'm glad to hear it, sir,' Tom mumbled, wondering where this conversation might be leading.

'I'm also informed that you volunteered for officer training and elected to go on active service and have put up a very good show in the recent fighting. But now I have a new commission for you.'

'A commission, sir?'

'Yes. I'm withdrawing you from front-line duties. I want you to paint a series of pictures – pictures that will show future generations what we lived through. I'm not laying down any specific requirements, only that your pictures should tell the truth about conditions in the trenches and about the courage and determination of the troops. You can have a room here as a studio, put in a requisition for whatever materials you need, and I will see that you have a pass allowing you to travel to any area of the conflict you may wish to record. Any questions?'

Tom stared at him wordlessly for a moment. The prospect of being reprieved from the horror of battle and allowed to spend his days doing the thing he loved most was almost too dazzling to contemplate, but at the same time his conscience told him it was cowardice.

'I'm sorry, sir,' he said. 'I can't accept.'

The general glared at him. 'What do you mean, "can't accept"? I've given you an order, dammit! You either obey it or you go before a court martial.'

'I'm not trying to be insubordinate, sir,' Tom said. 'It's just that it doesn't feel right for me to be painting pictures while other men are dying out there.'

The general's expression softened. 'It does you credit. But consider this: when this war is over, what are we going to be left with? Isn't it right that some good things should come out of it? You are an artist. Isn't it the role of the artist to transmute experience into something beautiful, even if the experience itself is . . . very far from beautiful?'

Tom remembered the Winged Victory in the Louvre and how his thoughts had run along exactly the same lines. After a moment he said, 'If you put it like that, sir, I can't argue. I'll do my best to fulfil the brief you have set out. But can I ask one thing?'

'Go ahead.'

'I'd like to make it a limited commitment, as far as time is concerned. When I feel I've done all I can do – or when I feel that I no longer have the necessary inspiration – will you let me return to my regiment?'

'Agreed. And I respect your scruples. I shan't come and look over your shoulder, but I'll look forward to seeing the results in a month or two. You might do worse than begin by painting this place.'

'I should like to do that,' Tom agreed. 'But I'm afraid very few of the pictures will be as . . . as pastoral as this.'

'I'll leave that to you,' Rawlinson said. 'You'd better have this sketch pad back, and I'll get someone to show you your room and you can get down to work.'

Halfway to the door, Tom turned back. 'Excuse me, sir. May I ask how you came by my sketch book?'

'It was passed on by your colonel. But I believe the originator of the idea was a friend of yours. Malham Brown, was that the name?'

Seven

Winter came early to the mountains of Macedonia, as Leo had predicted. There was no rapid breakthrough of the kind Sasha had envisaged. The Bulgarians and their Austrian allies held the high ground and were determined to defend it, but the

Serbs were not going to be denied this time. Ridge by ridge and mountain peak by mountain peak they forced the occupiers back. Supported by their French and British allies they hauled their guns up icy slopes and along snow-choked valleys, and at night they dug holes in the snow for shelter. And as they pressed forward, the Red Cross field hospital followed, setting up tents where they could find level ground or taking over the remains of buildings in the shattered villages. The personnel were a mixture of nationalities. The doctor in charge was a Frenchman named Pierre Leseaux; the chief nurse was a Scot, and under her were a Canadian, an Australian, two French girls and Leo.

As the weeks passed Leo was left in no doubt about her pregnancy. She was forced to let out the waistbands of her skirt and breeches and her uniform tunic no longer met over her stomach. Fortunately, she had equipped herself with a voluminous sheepskin coat before leaving Salonika and as she was huddled into that against the biting cold for most of the time her condition passed unnoticed for a while. She suffered very few of the ailments common in pregnancy, apart from a mild nausea first thing in the morning – a fact that she put down to having far too much to do to think about her own health. But this state of affairs could not last and one evening Patty, the Canadian, laid a hand on her arm.

'Leo, I know it's none of my business but you can't hide it any longer. You're pregnant, aren't you?'

'Yes, I am.'

'You shouldn't be here, working like this, in your condition.'

'I don't see why not. I'm perfectly healthy.'

'But suppose you had a fall or something. You could miscarry.'

'Well, I'm sure if that happened Doctor Pierre would be perfectly capable of dealing with it.'

'That isn't the point, is it? Or don't you want this baby? I mean, please don't think I'm judging you, but you're not married. Is that what this is all about?'

'No, it isn't!' Leo exclaimed, stung out of her calm. 'I want this baby very much – and so will its father, when he finds out.'

'When he finds out? Leo, is he out here, fighting? Is that why you're here?'

'Yes. But the fighting can't go on much longer. Not in the depths of winter.'

'I hope you're right. But I still think you should go back to Salonika.'

The following day Leo had a very similar conversation with Dr Leseaux, but nothing could persuade her to go back. Even to herself she could not explain why. She knew that for the sake of the child the safest place for her to be was in Salonika, and if Sasha knew what was happening he would certainly order her to go back; but some obstinate streak in her make-up made her determined to carry on and at the back of her mind always was the thought that if he were to be wounded she would be on hand to care for him.

On November the ninth the allied forces took the heights above the town of Bitola, forcing the Bulgarians to evacuate it. Leseaux's first action was to take over the hospital, where they found Bulgarian casualties, who had been too weak to go with the retreating army, left to fend for themselves. There were a few local nurses who had stayed at their posts during the occupation and others who came forward to volunteer as soon as they heard that the Bulgarians had gone, but with their own casualties to care for as well as the Bulgars the medical team was stretched to the limit. For several days Leo had no opportunity to enquire after Sasha, though she knew from reports brought by their own wounded that he was still alive and unhurt, somewhere in the mountains that surrounded the city. On some barely conscious level, she was relieved that their meeting was delayed. When she first realized she was pregnant she had looked forward to telling him and imagined that his delight and excitement would mirror her own, but now she recognized that the timing was far from opportune.

She had little time or energy to explore, but what she saw during brief forays in search of supplies surprised her. She had expected to find a small, dusty provincial town but now discovered a city of remarkable contrasts. North of the River Draga, the old Turkish town was a jumble of narrow streets crowding round two impressive mosques and a traditional covered market. To the south were broad boulevards lined with elegant houses, whose classical façades were ornamented with pretty balconies. Many of them bore plaques proclaiming that they housed the consulates of various foreign nations.

When Leo remarked on that fact to Leseaux he looked up with a smile. 'I know. Like you, I had never heard of Bitola but I have been talking to one of our Serbian friends. He told me that not so long ago this was the third largest city in southern Europe, after Constantinople and Salonika. It was an important crossroad for trade, you see. The Roman Via Egnatia passed through on its way to northern Europe, and another important route going from the Adriatic to Constantinople crossed it here. In the seventeenth and eighteenth centuries it was so important that many nations felt it necessary to have consulates here – hence the elegant buildings. And it was a cradle of Orthodox Christianity. When the Turks arrived there were so many monasteries in the surrounding hills that they gave it the name Monastir.'

'And now it's almost deserted, and being smashed to pieces,' Leo said. 'I wonder if it will ever recover.'

Bitola was under constant bombardment from Bulgarian artillery and from German planes. By Christmas there was scarcely a building in the city undamaged and even the hospital had been hit. With snow blocking the mountain passes it was impossible for supplies to get through from the south and rations began to run short. Working twelve-hour shifts on inadequate food, Leo's health began to suffer. Looking at herself in the mirror, on the rare occasions when she had time, she saw a haggard face with hollow cheeks, and sticklike arms and legs protruding from her swollen belly. She began to dread her encounter with Sasha more than ever.

Christmas passed, both the Western one and the Orthodox. Then one evening she was folding sheets in the tiny storeroom when she heard his voice behind her.

'Leo! Here you are! I've been searching for you.'

She put down the sheet she was holding and turned slowly to face him. For a split second she saw the happy anticipation on his face, then it faded to consternation and finally to anger.

'My God! What are you doing here in that condition?'

Leo took a deep breath. She longed to throw herself into his arms but the expression on his face froze her to the spot. 'My job,' she replied quietly. 'Like you.'

'Like me? The difference is I am not carrying a child!' They gazed at each other in silence for a few seconds. Then he went on: 'How long have you known?'

'Since . . . since just after you left Salonika.' It was only a small lie.

'And the child is due when?'

'I'm not sure. A month, six weeks . . .'

He made a gesture of incomprehension. 'What were you thinking of? How could you risk yourself, and the baby?'

'I wanted to be near you.' Her voice was shaking. 'And I hoped the campaign would be over much sooner . . . before the worst of the winter. I thought by now we would either be in Belgrade, or back in Salonika.'

He shook his head in disbelief. Then, at last, he came close to her and put his hands on her shoulders. 'You must go back.'

'I can't. Not until the spring comes. All the roads are closed. But I am in the right place, you see. This is a hospital, and Doctor Pierre is very competent . . . if he should be needed.'

'A hospital in a town that is being shelled every day! In a town that is running out of food! How could you be so stupid?'

Tears scalded her eyes. She moved to him and laid her head against his shoulder. 'Don't be angry, Sasha. I want you to be glad, for both of us. We are going to have a child . . . our child.'

'A child born out of wedlock,' he said. He did not draw back, but neither did he fold her in the embrace she craved.

She looked up at him. 'What does that matter? We are going to be married, one day.'

'One day. But that could be months, even years away. And the child is due long before that.'

'Why should we care? It doesn't matter to us.'

'But it will to other people. Even when we are married, to some people it will still be a bastard.'

The word struck her like a blow in the face. She drew back and stared at him.

He sighed deeply. 'I am responsible. This is my fault. I must take my share of the blame.'

'Don't look like that,' she begged. 'We should be rejoicing.'

He gazed at her bleakly. 'You have been completely irresponsible. You are risking your life, and the child's. I am afraid I can see very little to rejoice about. I'm sorry, I cannot . . . cannot . . .' He faltered, then turned about and left the room.

She called after him but he did not respond. She would have followed him, but her legs gave way under her and she sank down on to the pile of sheets and wept.

All the rest of the day she waited, expecting to hear his voice or his footsteps, convinced that when he had time to think he would come back and apologize and comfort her. But he did not come, and the next morning she learned that he had left at dawn to rejoin his troops.

Eight

The days passed and Leo continued to work at her usual tasks in spite of pleas from her colleagues to rest. Work was the only way she knew to stop herself brooding over her last conversation with Sasha. Then one day Dr Leseaux came into the ward where she was helping to serve the midday meal and drew her aside.

'It's bad news, Leo, I'm afraid. A message has just come in to say that Sasha has been wounded. We don't know how badly, but I am leaving immediately to fetch him. Try not to worry too much. It may be something relatively minor . . .'

'Where is he?'

'Lavci. It's a village in the mountains, a few miles away.'

Leo was taking off her apron. 'Give me two minutes. I'll get my coat.'

He shook his head. 'No, you are in no condition to go out

there in this weather. Wait here, and we will bring him back to you.'

Leo shook her head. 'I'm coming with you.'

He frowned. 'Leonora, I forbid you to risk yourself like this. Stay here.'

Leo's jaw set. 'You are not in a position to give me orders. If you refuse to take me with you I shall follow on horseback.' Then, in a different tone: 'Please, Pierre. We parted on bad terms. I must see him again. I couldn't bear to wait here, in case . . .' She left the sentence unfinished but they both knew what she meant.

He made a gesture of surrender. 'Very well. But wrap up warm . . .'

'I'll be back in a moment.'

It had snowed all morning and the oxen drawing the ambulance wagon plodded fetlock-deep, their breath steaming in the cold air. It seemed to Leo that they were scarcely moving up the narrow mountain road and she began to wish that she had carried out her threat and taken to horseback, though a residual thread of common sense told her that it would have been foolhardy in the extreme in her advanced state of pregnancy. The slow pace was driving her to distraction and she longed to seize the goad from the driver's hand and thrash the unresponsive beasts into a greater effort. Beside her, Patty, the Canadian nurse, took her hand and squeezed it.

'Try to keep calm. I'm sure his men are looking after him. We'll be there soon.'

As the wagon rocked and jolted Leo became aware of an intermittent pain in her abdomen. She wondered vaguely what she might have eaten to cause it.

The winter evening was closing in as they came to a small village in a steep-sided valley. All along the route they had heard the sound of the guns drawing closer but with darkness falling the firing had stopped and camp fires were beginning to flicker around the outskirts. The air smelt of gun- and wood smoke. As the wagon drew up in the village square the door of the largest house opened and a man, whom Leo recognized as one of Sasha's officers, came out. Leseaux jumped down and the man crossed quickly to meet him.

As she clambered clumsily down from the wagon, Leo caught snatches of their conversation. 'Wasted journey . . . mortally wounded . . . had to leave him . . . overrun by the enemy . . . too late anyway . . .'

She slid down to the ground and as she did so the pain in her stomach returned with a violence that convulsed her. 'What are you saying?' she gasped. 'Where is Colonel Malkovic?'

The officer turned and she saw the shock on his face as he recognized her. For a moment he seemed unable to speak, then he blurted out: 'There was nothing we could do. I'm sorry. The colonel is dead.'

Leo stared at him and said the first thing that came into her head: 'He can't be! I'm carrying his child.' Then the pain came again and she doubled over with a choking cry.

Leseaux gripped her shoulders. '*Mon dieu!* Is it the child? Are you in labour?'

She gazed into his face helplessly. She had nursed men in all sorts of conditions but her knowledge of the process of childbirth was almost non-existent. 'I don't know . . . I . . .' Then another spasm of pain swept through her.

After that her comprehension of what was happening around her was cloudy. All her attention was turned inwards, to the extraordinary activity of her own muscles, which were following their own predetermined programme independent of her will. She was dimly aware of being half-led, half-carried into the house; of being laid on a bed while Patty pulled off her boots and stockings; of hands touching and pressing in ways she had never experienced before and of being examined with an intimacy that would have horrified her a day earlier. None of it mattered. Only the pain was real – and the pain went on and grew to a climax and then faded and then returned again, stronger than ever.

Time grew meaningless. Oil lamps and candles were lit around her. Then she must have slept, or lost consciousness for a while, because she opened her eyes to the pale light of a winter dawn. Patty was leaning over her, sponging her face and murmuring words of encouragement, and from time to time Leseaux appeared and examined her. The pain grew to a climax again and voices urged her to 'Push! Push hard now!'

She bore down as hard as she could but nothing happened. She could hear voices, too far away to distinguish what they said but she recognized the tone. It was the tone doctors and nurses used when a patient was in a critical condition. She made out the words 'weak' and 'exhausted'.

Then Leseaux appeared again in her line of vision. 'Leo, you are having a difficult labour and the child may be in distress. We have to help you, but first I am going to give you chloroform. Soon the pain will be over.'

The pad was laid over her nose and mouth and she briefly smelt the familiar scent of chloroform. Then came the merciful descent into oblivion.

She was being moved. There was still pain, but of a different sort. She could feel the sway and jolting of the ox-cart. Two thoughts surfaced in her brain. Sasha was dead – and she had given birth to his child. Or had she?

'My baby?' she croaked through parched lips. 'Where is my baby?'

Patty lifted her head and held a cup to her lips. 'Don't worry. Your baby's fine. Just fine.'

Leo sank back. The drink must have contained a sedative, for she lost consciousness again.

The next time she opened her eyes it was evening and she was in bed in a room she recognized as a side ward in the hospital at Bitola. Nausea welled up in her throat, and she rolled on to her side and was sick. When the spasm had passed she heard voices outside and called out, her voice hoarse and feeble. Patty came in.

'I'm sorry. I've been . . .'

'Don't worry about it. I'll soon have that cleared up.' Patty sat on the edge of the bed and took her hand. 'Welcome back. You had us worried for a while, back there.'

'My baby?' Leo whispered. 'I want to see my baby.'

'Don't worry about her. She's being looked after.'

'Her?'

'You had a little girl. Not so little, either. That's why you had so much trouble producing her. Now, I bet you're thirsty. Here . . .' She held Leo's head while she drank, then went on:

'Now, I'll go get a mop to clear this mess up. You just lie back and rest.'

Shortly afterwards Leseaux came in. He took Leo's pulse and felt her forehead. 'You have a slight fever, but that's not surprising. You need to rest.'

'When can I see my baby?' Leo begged.

He sat beside her. 'Leo, when your child was born you were in no condition to look after her. And we had no means of feeding her. But by chance a woman in the village had just given birth to a stillborn child. It was by the grace of *le Bon Dieu, ma chère.* She agreed to take the child.'

'You gave my baby away!'

'No, no! We explained that you would return as soon as you were strong enough, to collect her. And I left something with her, something that will prove in the future who she is, in case there should ever be a question.'

'What? What did you leave?'

'I left the locket you have always worn round your neck. You told me once that it was given to you by Sasha. I looked inside and saw that it is inscribed with his family motto. I hope you will forgive me. I know it meant a lot to you, but I thought, under the circumstances . . . She is a good woman, Leo. She has three children of her own already; all strong and healthy. She will take good care of your little Alexandra until you come for her.'

'Alexandra?'

'You told me once that you wanted your child to be named after its father.'

The mention of Sasha sent a stab like a physical wound through Leo. She turned her face into the pillow. 'He's dead! Sasha's dead and you have given his child away to strangers!'

She was dimly aware of his repeated assurances that she could fetch the child as soon as she was strong enough, but her sobs drowned out his voice. There was movement around her, then the sharp stab of a hypodermic needle and silence.

When she woke again it was dark and the fog of pain and exhaustion was beginning to lift. The same two thoughts crystallized in her brain: Sasha was dead and his child – their child – had been abandoned to the care of strangers. What was worse, to strangers who lived in a village that was at the centre of a battle. As she brooded on that, a new thought came to her. It was all her own fault! Sasha had been right to be angry with her. She had left Salonika in the full knowledge that she was pregnant. Leseaux had tried to persuade her to return but she had refused. Then she had insisted on going with him to find Sasha, although she had known her time was near. It was her own obstinacy, her own stupid determination to have things her own way, that had resulted in the loss of her baby. Arrogant – that was how her grandmother had described her, all those years ago. And she had been right!

Leo dragged herself into a sitting position, suppressing a cry as pain stabbed upwards from her vagina. The first faint light of dawn was visible through the window. She swung her legs carefully over the edge of the bed and dragged herself upright. For a moment she swayed, then regained her balance and staggered over to a cupboard in the corner. Relief surged through her as she discovered that her clothes were in it, as she had hoped. Even the thick woollen scarf she had wrapped round her throat before she left, and the evil-smelling sheepskin coat were there. She began to pull them on. Her baby had been left with strangers because of her stupidity. Well, it was up to her to put that right.

It took her some time to dress. From time to time she had to sit down on the edge of the bed to recover from spells of dizziness, but she managed it eventually. She opened the door of her room cautiously. In the ward the curtains were still closed and the only light came from an oil lamp on the desk of the duty nurse at the far end. The nurse herself was busy sewing, her head bent close to the work, and she did not look up as Leo crept out of the ward. The corridor was silent but Leo knew that within minutes it would be loud with the noise of rattling trolleys and cheery voices. She padded softly in her fur-lined boots to the door that led to the courtyard outside and unlocked it, holding her breath at the sound of the big key turning.

The icy air almost took her breath away, but the yard had been swept clear of snow. She had to feel her way along the wall to stop herself from falling, but she made it to the door of the stable where Leseaux's gelding and her own little mare were kept. Star greeted her with a soft whinny and Leo laid her arm across the horse's withers and clung there, soaking up her warmth, until her strength returned. It took her a long time, with numb, shaking fingers, to put the bridle on and the weight of the saddle almost defeated her, but Star was quiet and easy to manage and she succeeded in the end. She led the horse out into the yard and over to a mounting block. Previously she would have scorned such assistance but now, even with it, the effort of mounting seemed insuperable. As she hauled herself up her whole body screamed with pain and once in the saddle she slumped forward over the horse's neck. Her body was too bruised and torn to sit upright.

She clicked her tongue and the horse walked forward, out through the arched entrance to the courtyard and into the still sleeping street. Slowly they picked their way past the rubble of bombed buildings and Leo wondered how much time she had before the daily bombardment began again. She almost forgot that every street leading into the city was guarded until a sentry stepped out in front of her to demand a password.

With a supreme effort Leo forced herself to sit upright. 'You know me! I've been called to attend a woman in childbirth. Let me pass.'

Fortunately, the first statement was true. The English lady nurse was a familiar sight in the city and the man let her go without further question. She was stopped three more times as she made her way through the outlying houses, but the same formula got her through.

Out on the open road the wind cut into her like a scythe. It had frozen hard overnight and the packed snow on the road had turned to ice, on which the horse's hooves slid and skittered. Leo clung to the mane, her head swimming. The sun rose, red, above the eastern mountains, and as if it were a signal the enemy guns opened up. Shells thundered and whistled over them and the mare threw up her head and tried to turn back. Leo battled with the reins, which were stiff with cold. Then a shell exploded only a few yards away, showering them both with shards of ice that cut like glass. The mare reared, Leo lost her grip and fell sideways into one of the deep drifts of snow that lined the road.

Nine

Winter had the fields and cities of Northern France in its grip, too. On the exposed hilltop where the Calais Convoy was encamped temperatures dropped to below zero every night and in the morning all the cars were frozen up and impossible to start. Lilian Franklin came to the conclusion that there was only one solution: every car must be started once every hour, right through the night. A rota was set up and for the FANYs who were on duty each night there was very little sleep.

Victoria stumbled off to bed at dawn after a night of cranking recalcitrant motors, hoping that there would not be an emergency that would require all the available ambulances. It seemed that she had scarcely closed her eyes before there was a knock on her door and Wilks looked in.

'Sorry, old thing. Something's come up and Boss wants you, on the double.'

Victoria dragged on her boots and her overcoat and plodded across the compound to Franklin's office, her drowsy brain registering two facts: one, that all the ambulances except her own were absent, so presumably a barge or a hospital train had come in, and two, it was beginning to snow.

Franklin greeted her briskly. 'Sorry to drag you out of bed but we've had a call from army HQ. A car carrying two high-ranking officers has crashed on the road from Saint Omer, just the far side of Ardres, and the driver has been injured. They want us to send an ambulance to pick them up. You and Wilks are the only ones left in camp and you are the better driver, so I'm sending you. Take care. The roads are very treacherous.'

Victoria cranked her converted Napier's engine into life and climbed into the driving seat. The snow was coming down harder than ever and the road down the hill was as slippery as an ice rink. The car had no windscreen, and the snowflakes stung her face and caked on her eyelashes until it was almost impossible to keep her eyes open. She tried putting on her goggles, but the snow settled on them and rapidly obscured her vision. She found that the only solution was to drive with one eye open while she rubbed at the other to clear it. Soon both her hands were frozen, in spite of her fur-lined leather gloves, and her feet were so cold that she could hardly feel the pedals.

The main road towards St Omer was hardly any better. The constant passing of heavy lorries, and more recently tanks, had broken up the pavé and churned the surface into ruts, which had now frozen hard as concrete and the ambulance skidded and bounced over them. In addition, there were frequent craters from bombs or shells to be negotiated. On either side, the road was lined with the snow-shrouded shapes of burnt-out vehicles and dead horses. Once through Ardres and closer to the front line conditions were even worse. Victoria's eyes were streaming with the effort of seeing ahead through the driving snow and her shoulders ached with the struggle to keep the car on the road.

Suddenly, above the noise of the engine she heard another sound, a rushing, rattling noise coming closer; then there was a loud explosion a few yards ahead of her. Snow and debris shot up in the air and a second later the blast wave hit the car, wrenching the steering wheel out of her hands. The car skidded, bounced, and toppled over into the ditch. The impact broke the ice, immersing Victoria in the freezing water beneath. She struggled to get her head clear, gasping for air, and realized that she was trapped inside. With numb fingers she grabbed the metal struts that supported the hood and tried to haul herself out, only to be brought up short by a tearing pain in her lower leg. Looking down, she saw that the muddy water was being further darkened by a spreading stain. Her leg was trapped under some part of the chassis and although she gritted her teeth and heaved with all her might she could not free it.

The cold was penetrating through her clothes and into the core of her body. It numbed the pain in her leg but she knew that unless she was rescued soon she would die, either from exposure or from loss of blood. She drew a deep breath and shouted for help, but the road, often crowded with traffic, was uncannily silent. It struck her that she had not passed another vehicle, going in either direction, for several miles.

How long she hung there she did not know, but when she was almost at the end of her strength and beginning to slip in and out of consciousness she became aware of a regular crunching sound getting closer and closer. It took a moment for her to realize that it was the sound of army boots marching through snow. She summoned her last strength and shouted for help. The boots came closer and she could hear whistling. She shouted again, but the boots kept marching without a break in the rhythm. In desperation she thrashed at the water with arms that were almost too numb to move and screamed again.

Then, at last, she heard the regular steps break. Voices approached and a face peered down at her. 'Cor blimey! It's a woman. How long you been down there? Hold on, luv. We'll have you out of there in two ticks. Come on, lads. Lay hold! Heave! Heave!'

A dozen hands hauled at the body of the ambulance and others gripped Victoria's shoulders. She screamed with pain as the weight was lifted from her leg and she was dragged out of the ditch. The concerned faces surrounding her blurred and she lost consciousness.

Victoria came round in the familiar surroundings of the Casino Hospital. Beryl Hutchinson was sitting by her bed.

'Hello, old thing. I say, you have been in the wars! What happened?'

'I was going to ask you that,' Victoria mumbled.

'All I know is you were found in a ditch underneath Nellie, up to your neck in cold water.'

Victoria searched her memory. 'Oh, Lord! I was supposed to pick up some top-notch brass hats. What happened to them?'

'Oh, don't worry about them. From what I've heard they were picked up by an army convoy heading in this direction and were back in Calais soon after you set out. You must have passed them on the way.'

'Wonderful!' Victoria muttered. 'They might have given me a wave.' Her chest hurt every time she drew a breath and her leg was throbbing as if someone was hitting it with a large hammer. She lifted her head and peered down the bed. A cage had been placed under the blankets to keep them off her legs and a sudden dreadful thought struck her. 'Is it still there?'

'Is what still there?'

'My leg. Both my legs?'

Hutchinson gave a little gasp. 'Bless you! Of course they are. Can't you feel them?'

'Oh, yes, I can feel them all right,' Victoria responded grimly. 'But that's what happens when . . . when they take them off, isn't it? It feels as if they are still there.'

'All right. To set your mind at rest, I'll take a look.' Hutchinson went to the end of the bed and lifted the blankets. 'All present and correct. Do you want me to count your toes?'

Victoria sank back on her pillows with a sigh of relief. 'No, thanks. I'll take the toes on trust.'

An hour or two later the same doctor who had set her arm came to examine her. 'Not you again!' he said. 'I patched you up last time. You're a glutton for punishment, and no mistake.'

'How bad is it?' Victoria asked.

'It's a nasty break. We had to operate and there was a moment when we thought we might not be able to save the leg, but it should heal satisfactorily, given time. You're going to be out of action for quite a while, though. Are you in much pain? Do you want a shot of morphine?'

'It's not the leg, so much,' Victoria wheezed. 'My chest hurts.'

The doctor took out his stethoscope and listened to her chest for some time. When he removed the instrument from his ears his face was grave.

'Yes, I'm not surprised it's painful. We're going to have to look after you very carefully, young lady.'

By which Victoria understood that she was seriously ill.

Luke Pavel watched the coast of France materialize slowly out of the grey mist of sky and sea.

'Bit of a change after Gallipoli,' commented the man standing next to him.

'Don't think we're going to have to worry about sunburn,' Luke agreed.

'Or flies. That's what really got me down on the last show. Bloody flies over everything. You couldn't put a bite of food in your mouth without getting flies in with it.'

'You don't have to remind me,' Luke said with a shudder.

'Let's hope the natives are friendly,' his companion said.

'Well, I don't think they'll be taking pot shots at us when we land this time,' Luke said. 'But don't let's get too optimistic. This isn't going to be a picnic.'

'It can't be as bad as Gallipoli.'

'You want to bet?'

After a night in barracks in Calais the Wellingtons were ordered to form fours and marched out of the city and down the long, straight road towards Ypres. The snow had melted, the ditches at each side were overflowing and the Flemish polders were underwater.

Luke's friend looked around him. 'People actually live here?'

'Reckon so.'

'Guess they must be born with webbed feet, then.'

At the end of the third day's march they reached their allotted position. For miles they had tramped through the carnage of earlier battles. The landscape was a sea of mud, churned up by tank tracks and pitted with shell-holes. Here and there the skeletal remains of a tree stuck up, or the crumbling walls of a building. They had heard the guns as a distant, background rumble from the moment they disembarked, but now it was a constant, ear-shattering cacophony, punctuated by the whistle of the smaller shells and the express-train thunder of the big ones.

An English sergeant directed them off the road and down some steps into a communications trench, where they were up to their knees in water. They squelched along for almost a mile until they reached the reserve trench, where an Australian battalion, waiting to be relieved, greeted them with grim humour and welcomed them to the dugouts they had been inhabiting. Later, on sentry duty, Luke found himself standing next to his company lieutenant, who was examining the surroundings through a periscope. 'Anything to see out there, sir?' he asked.

'Sod all, except mud,' the officer replied. 'Have a look for yourself.'

Luke peered through the periscope, swinging it in a slow arc from west to east. Away across the level plain he saw a low, curving ridge and the outlines of a small village. 'What's that place called?' he asked.

The lieutenant consulted his map.

'Not sure how you pronounce it. 'Pass . . . Passchysomething . . . See for yourself.'

Luke looked over his shoulder. Passchendaele, he read.

Leo was watching a thin line of sunlight moving across the ceiling above her bed. It moved slowly from right to left and then back again, and as it did so she felt the weight of her own body shift from one side to the other. The sensation puzzled her. The ox-carts never swayed with this gentle, rocking motion – and anyway, she had been on horseback. She had been riding . . . riding where? It was important. She had been on an important mission. Where was she going? She must remember.

She moved and a stab of pain in her lower body stopped her short. She was hurt. Why? Something had happened . . . Then memory flooded back, with the same two agonizing thoughts. Sasha was dead, and their child had been abandoned. She had to find her child! She sat up and cracked her head on something immediately above her. She was lying in a bunk, and suddenly she understood why the light kept moving. She was on a ship. But a ship would not take her to where her child was. How had she come here? Was she a prisoner?

She sat up again, more cautiously, and was about to slide out of the bunk when the door opened and Patty came in, carrying a tray.

'Hey, where do you think you're going?' she exclaimed. 'Come on, now. Back into bed. You've been very ill. Just lie back and take it easy. I'll get you anything you want.'

'Where are we going?' Leo demanded, her voice a husky whisper. 'Why are we on a ship?'

'You're going home,' Patty said. 'And I'm coming with you. I've always wanted to see England.'

'England?' Leo repeated. 'What do you mean? I don't want to go to England.'

'It's the best place for you, believe me,' Patty said gently. 'You are going to need a long period of rest and recuperation. And you need to be with your own people, your own family.'

'I don't have a family!' Leo protested. 'I have a brother, but he's fighting in France, if he's still alive. My family is in Serbia. Sasha was my family. Now that he's dead all I have left is my child. I have to find her. Patty, you must tell them to turn the ship round. I have to go back to Salonika.'

Patty laughed, but there were tears in her eyes. 'You don't understand, my dear. This isn't a private yacht. It's a Royal Naval hospital ship, taking casualties back to England. The captain isn't going to turn around on your say-so. Anyway, we've been at sea for two days now. It's too far to go back.'

'Two days?' Leo murmured. 'How can that be? I was at Bitola yesterday. I was going to find my baby.'

'Not yesterday, sweetheart. It's a week since we found you half-buried in a snow drift. We wouldn't have had any idea where to look if your little mare hadn't come cantering back into the yard. I can't believe you actually got up on her and stayed on that long, after what you had been through with the birth! We thought you were dead when we found you, but there was still just a little spark. Doctor Pierre wrapped you in his own cloak and carried you in his arms all the way back to the hospital. The next day the thaw started – you know how sudden this can be in the mountains – and when the road was open it was decided that you would be better off back in Salonika. We got there just in time to catch this ship and I got the job of taking care of you. The doctors agreed it would be better for you to have one familiar face around.'

'And I've been unconscious all this time?'

'Not completely. You've surfaced from time to time, but never really been aware of where you were. I guess our bodies, or our minds maybe, know when we just need some time out, time for the healing process to begin.'

'But my child . . .' Leo said.

'Listen to me. The woman who took your baby in is a good person. Everyone in the village vouched for that. She was grieving for her stillborn baby and she was happy to be given yours to care for. She will look after her, I promise you that. And Doctor Pierre left some money to help with her expenses. But it was made absolutely clear that it was only a temporary arrangement, that one day you would come to claim the child. When you are stronger, and when circumstances allow, you can go back and find her.'

'What is her name – the woman who took my child?'

'Popovic. That's the family name. I never heard her first name.'

'What did you mean, "when circumstances allow"?'

Patty hesitated. 'That was one reason why it was decided that you should go home. The day after we found you we heard that the village had been retaken by the Bulgarians. You may have to wait for the war to be over before you can go back.'

Leo closed her eyes. 'Wait for the war to be over . . .' she murmured. 'I feel as if I have spent most of my life waiting for that.'

Patty was silent for a moment, then Leo heard a rustle as she took something from her pocket.

'Leo, you said that you and Sasha parted on bad terms . . .'

'He was angry with me for letting myself get pregnant. No, not really that . . . For not staying in Salonika. For putting myself and the child at risk . . . He was right, of course. I've only myself to blame.'

'I'm not sure if this is the right moment . . .' Patty hesitated, then held out an envelope. 'A messenger brought this to the hospital on the day we found you in the snow. Apparently Sasha wrote it just before he was killed.' She laid the envelope on the bed. 'I'll leave you alone to read it. If you want anything, just call. I won't be far away.'

Leo took up the envelope. It was creased and stained, but the writing was unmistakable. Had he written to reinforce the criticisms he had made on their last meeting? Was this a letter of rejection, informing her that he had changed his mind and wanted nothing more to do with her? For a moment she was tempted to tear it up, unread. But whatever it said, it was his last word to her. However painful, she must read it. With fingers that shook uncontrollably, she slit the envelope and read:

My dearest love,

I am writing this in case I am not able to come to you in person to apologize for my cruel and selfish behaviour. How can I begin? The way I treated you was unforgivable. In my defence I can only say that I was in a state of shock – not at the fact of your pregnancy but at the sight of you, my dearest one, so thin and worn. All I could think of was the terrible risk you were taking with your health and I was terrified that the birth of the child might be too much for you. I could not bear to lose you, my heart's companion.

Of course, I rejoice in the thought that we are to have a child and, as you said yourself, what does it matter that we are not married? Let people think what they will – we know that we have been wedded to each other in our hearts since the day an improbably beautiful 'boy' saved my life at Chataldzha. I have rewritten my will in the last few hours and had it duly witnessed. In it, I repudiate my marriage to Eudoxie on the grounds of non-consummation and declare you to be my affianced bride. If I should die here, my estate is to go to our son, or daughter. I have made due provision for Eudoxie so that she will not suffer financially through my action and I truly believe it will come as a relief to her. We could never have made a successful marriage.

All this may be unnecessary. God willing, I shall be back in Bitola before the child is born and able to beg your forgiveness in person. If you can bring yourself to accept my abject apology we can rejoice together in the birth and look forward to the time when we can take our child home to Belgrade. But you must take care of yourself. You are more fragile than you know. I have written to Dr Leseaux, begging him to persuade you to rest.

I pray that you may never read this letter. But if it should

*happen, know that I love you more than all the world. I would
give the whole of Serbia to assure your safety, and that of our
child.*

Take care of yourself, wife of my heart.
Your loving husband,
Sasha

Ten

Tom came to attention in front of the general's desk and saluted.
'I have a request, sir.'

Rawlinson pushed back his chair and removed his pipe from
his mouth. 'I think I can guess what it is. You want me to
keep my promise and send you back to the front line.'

'Yes, sir. I've finished the last painting and I feel that there
is no more I can say in the form of pictures, at least for the
time being. And now that spring is here there is bound to be
a new campaign. I can't lurk here while other men are fighting
and dying.'

'From what I hear you haven't exactly been lurking, as you
put it,' the general said with a quiet smile. 'You seem to have
spent as much time up at the front as you have in your studio.
Not that I am criticizing. The results speak for themselves.'

'But I've been there as an observer,' Tom said. 'I haven't
shared the danger, or the discomfort, for more than a few days
at a time.'

'Well, your desire to return to that danger and discomfort
does you credit, and I'm not going to break my promise. But
there is one thing I want you to do first.'

'What is that, sir?'

'I want people back home to see your pictures. I want them
to know the reality of the conditions out here and what is
being done and suffered in their names. I've spoken to one
or two people who have more expertise in this area than I
do and as a result I have been able to arrange for your work
to be exhibited at the Albemarle Gallery. I want you to go

back to London with the paintings and make sure they are hung to their best advantage. After that, you will be free to return to your unit. Happy with that?'

Happy! Tom struggled to find words. To have a one-man show at a prestigious London gallery was something he had never even dreamed of. He swallowed hard. 'Yes, sir. Very happy indeed. Thank you.'

'Good.' Rawlinson got up and stretched himself. 'There's a train leaving for Calais the day after tomorrow. I've arranged for a special truck to be attached to accommodate your paintings. After that, I've organized onward transport to London. That gives you two days to get all the work crated up ready. All except one picture. I want to buy that from you. It's the painting of this place. I'd like to have that as a souvenir. I don't know what you normally price your work at, but I've made out a cheque.' He took out his pocket book and handed Tom the slip of paper, made out for a sum that almost made him gasp aloud. 'Is that acceptable?'

'Oh, yes, sir! Very acceptable. More than generous, in fact.'

'Good. And once the exhibition is over you will be free to sell the rest of the work at whatever price you and the gallery owner feel is appropriate. Now, can you be ready in time? Have a word with the quartermaster. I'm sure he can find you a couple of chippies to do the work and provide whatever you need in the way of timber, etc. Can you do it?'

'Yes, I suppose so.' Tom had a feeling that it would be a close thing, but it must be done somehow. 'Yes, of course.'

'Right. You can travel with the pictures. I'll get the adjutant to make out the necessary dockets. Take a bit of leave while you're over there. Will two weeks be enough for what you need?'

Once again, Tom was at a loss. He had no idea how long it took to set up an exhibition, but he felt he could not ask for more.

'That's settled, then.' Rawlinson nodded affably. 'Send my picture down to me, will you? I shall enjoy looking at it in moments of stress. Nice to feel that something worthwhile has come out of this shambles.'

Two days later the crates containing the pictures were

loaded on to a lorry to be taken to the railhead. Tom looked back as they drove away and experienced a sudden flood of gratitude. For nearly six months he had been spared the worst horrors of the war, but it had been a time when his emotions had swung from one extreme to the other. There had been days, painting in the airy room at the top of the chateau which had been given to him as a studio, when he had ceased to hear the distant, perpetual thunder of the guns and had been possessed by a sense of the rightness of his situation; that he was at last doing what nature, or God, intended him to do. Then there had been times, venturing up to the front to sketch new images of the conflict, when he was consumed with guilt. Once, when he was packing up his gear to return to the chateau, a fellow officer had remarked scathingly, 'Off back to your funkhole, are you?' The remark had stung and lingered in Tom's mind long after he had forgotten who said it.

He had seen Ralph three times over the six-month period. Twice he had managed to catch up with him when his battalion was in reserve billets behind the line, but he had been distracted and on edge, drinking heavily and unable to sustain a conversation for longer than a minute or two. But then Ralph had been given forty-eight hours' leave and had come to find him at the chateau. There was no spare accommodation, so they had shared a room and, for the first time since the incident with the boy, Louis, they recaptured some of their old schoolboy comradeship. Tom had reconciled himself to the idea that Ralph had desires which he would have been only too happy to satisfy, but that he had been cast in an idealized role that made any thought of that impossible. Ralph loved him like a brother, and that would have to suffice.

Ralph had admired the pictures and said with a grin, 'I knew I was doing the right thing.'

'You engineered this, didn't you?' Tom asked. 'But how did you manage it?'

Ralph tapped the side of his nose conspiratorially. 'Old boy network. 'Nuff said?'

Now, heading away from the chateau, Tom wondered if he had been a fool. Probably he could have strung out the painting for another month or two, and by then there would have been another 'big push' which would bring the final victory. Everyone said it must come this summer. But he knew that if he had done that he would have felt diminished in his own eyes, if not in the eyes of the world.

The crates were loaded into the goods van, which had been attached to the troop train, and Tom settled himself in a First Class, Officers Only compartment. His three companions, who were all considerably higher in rank than himself, talked among themselves and seemed to regard him as an interloper. Used to the snobbery of the regular army, Tom opened a magazine and ignored them.

The train was half way to Calais when it jolted to a sudden halt and whistles began to blow all along its length. 'Enemy aircraft! Take cover! Take cover!' Tom grabbed his tin hat and peered out of the window. There was a roar and a German Fokker biplane skimmed low over the train. Tom could see the pilot and in the rear cockpit the gunner, sighting his machine gun. White puffs of smoke blossomed around it from the anti-aircraft guns mounted on a flat truck at the rear of the train. Then came a rattle like heavy hailstones as bullets swept the train from front to rear. Tom ducked back sharply and joined the other officers crouched on the floor of the compartment. They heard the plane's engine scream as it pulled up at the end of its traverse, then the increasing noise as it returned for a second sweep. This time there were no bullets, but two explosions rocked the carriages.

As the sound of the plane's engine faded away a new cry went up. 'Fire! Fire!'

Tom leapt out of the compartment and ran back towards the rear of the train. The German pilot had dropped his bombs with remarkable accuracy, presumably thinking that the closed truck at the rear contained weapons or other items of war material. They must have been incendiaries, because the whole truck was ablaze. Men were swarming round it with stirrup pumps but Tom could see at once that it was pointless. There was nothing he could do but watch as the work of six months, the pictures that might have established his reputation, went up in smoke.

★   ★   ★

When the fire had been put out the train proceeded on its way and Tom went with it. There seemed little point in doing otherwise. By the following day he was in London. Standing on the platform, surrounded by ecstatic scenes of returning servicemen being greeted by their loved ones, he was undecided about where to go. There was no reason to stay in town, now that he had no exhibition to arrange. He had the telephone number of the gallery owner in his diary, so he went to a phone booth and called it. The man was aghast at the cancellation of the plans and seemed more concerned with his own loss than with Tom's, so Tom brought the conversation to a rapid conclusion.

He still had to decide where to spend his leave. His house in Cheyne Walk was let for the duration and the prospect of checking into a hotel did not appeal. He reminded himself that he had not seen his parents since he'd finished his officer training, over a year earlier. He had not enjoyed that leave and his heart sank at the thought of repeating the experience, but he felt duty-bound to make the effort. So he crossed London to Marylebone Station and took a train for Denham. It was late April and the beech trees were flaunting their new green leaves, while the understory was carpeted with white wood anemones. Watching the scenery slip past, Tom was possessed by a wave of nostalgia for boyhood wanderings and reminded that his childhood had not been entirely bleak. He hired a pony and trap at the station to take him to the Hall and as they drove through the gates he was struck by the air of neglect. Weeds were growing up through the gravel and the lawns were untrimmed, and as he drew closer he saw that the paintwork around the window frames was peeling. He knew labour was short, because of the war, but he was surprised that things had been allowed to deteriorate to this extent.

The door was opened by Lowndes, the family butler, and Tom was shaken to see how much he had aged since his last visit. He could never remember him being a young man, but now his hair was completely white and the hand that held the door open shook slightly. Tom had not given any warning of his arrival, which perhaps accounted for the expression of something close to alarm that crossed the old man's face when he recognized him.

'We weren't expecting you, sir. Sir George is in London, at his club, but Her Ladyship is upstairs in her boudoir. If you'll wait in the drawing room, I'll tell her you are here.'

Tom thought of the scenes he had witnessed at Victoria station, but reminded himself that he had not let anyone know he was on his way back, so he could scarcely complain that no one had come to meet him. Nevertheless, he could not dismiss a lingering feeling that even if he had told his parents it would not have made a material difference. He went into the drawing room and stopped short. Above the mantelpiece an oblong of unfaded wallpaper, edged by a line of dust, stood out starkly.

Tom swung round to address the butler's departing back. 'Lowndes, what's happened to the Stubbs?'

The old man turned back, his shoulders drooping. 'Sold, I believe, sir. A matter of paying off a gambling debt.'

Tom drew a deep breath. So, his father's gambling addiction was getting worse, apparently. He felt sorry for the old butler, who had served the family for so long. 'Thank you, Lowndes. That is all.'

When the man had gone Tom looked around the room and quickly realized that the painting was not the only thing missing. Two smaller watercolours had vanished, as had a silver rose bowl and a Chinese vase. He began to see the room as a stranger might and noticed that the furniture was dusty and the carpet worn threadbare in places. His sense of disquiet deepened.

Lowndes returned. 'Her Ladyship asks you to go up, sir.'

No rush to embrace the returning soldier here, then! Tom climbed the stairs and found his mother sitting at her embroidery frame in a room cluttered with examples of her work. Cross-stitched cushions were heaped on every chair, pictures were thrown over the backs, table runners and bell-pulls were scattered on every other surface. The evidence, he saw for the first time, not of a hobby, but of an obsessive escape from reality.

His mother looked up from her work but did not put down her needle. 'Good afternoon, Thomas. I hope you are well.'

He walked over and kissed her on the cheek. 'Well enough, Mother, thank you. And you? How are you?'

'Oh, much as usual. Have you eaten? Would you like some tea?'

'Later, perhaps.' He tipped some of her work off a chair and set it close to her. 'Mother, I want to ask you something. Did you know that the Stubbs painting has been sold – and some other things as well?'

She bent her head closer to her sewing and answered indistinctly, 'I believe your father needed some money. He owed it to some bookies.'

'He's still gambling, then. How bad is it?'

She shook her head. 'I don't know about these things.'

Tom reached out and took her hands, stilling the obsessive movement of her needle. 'When was father last here?'

'I . . . don't remember. It was Christmas, I think. Yes, there was a party . . . a lot of noise.'

'A party! Up to his ears in debt, and he's still throwing parties! And he hasn't been down here since then?'

'No, I . . . I don't think so.'

He leaned closer, gripping her hands, forcing her to look at him. 'Mother, how bad are things really? You must have some idea.'

She closed her eyes, as if trying to shut out a thought. Then she said, almost in a whisper, 'John Standing was here the other day. He wanted to talk to me about selling off some land. He was saying something about the bank, and a mortgage. I told him there is nothing I can do. Your father is the only one who can deal with these things.'

Tom sat back and took a deep breath. He knew Standing, the estate manager, for an honest, sensible man. If he was worried enough to want to sell land, affairs must have reached a critical state. He looked at his mother, seeing her now not as the cold, unloving figure of his childhood but as a pathetic woman who had shut herself off in order to escape from an unhappy marriage. He patted her hand. 'Don't worry. I'll see Standing in the morning and then I'll go up to town and talk to father.'

At a meeting the next day with the estate manager and Mr

Featherstone, the family solicitor, Tom was made fully aware of how desperate the situation was. His father had mortgaged the estate to fund his alcoholism and his gambling and now the bank was threatening to foreclose on the debt. Bills for wine and groceries remained unpaid, staff had been dismissed and for those that were left wages were months in arrears. And to add to that there was the unknown amount that might be owing to bookmakers.

'I'll be frank with you, Lieutenant Devenish,' Featherstone said. 'Unless something is done soon we shall have the bailiffs in.'

As soon as the meeting was over Tom took the train to London and made his way to his father's club. A steward informed him stiffly that Sir George was not on the premises at present but was expected back that evening. Meanwhile, he suggested, the club secretary would like a word with him.

It was just as Tom expected: a catalogue of complaints about unpaid bar bills and drunken confrontations with other members.

'To be frank with you, Lieutenant,' the secretary said, 'unless you can see your way clear to settle the outstanding bill I am afraid we shall have to ask Sir George to leave – and it may even come to a matter of involving the police.'

'I understand,' Tom said. 'How much is owing?'

The secretary handed him a bill and Tom reached for his cheque book with a sigh. It was almost exactly the same amount as the general had paid him for his picture.

'Do you know where my father is at the moment?'

'He has gone to Newmarket for the races, I believe.'

Tom shook his head in disbelief. He knew, from conversations in the mess, of the crazy conviction of the inveterate gambler that one last lucky bet would solve all his problems, but he found it hard to credit that any sane man could believe it. But then, he was beginning to wonder if his father was sane. He waited in the bar for him to return. Sir George came in just before dinner and from the tone of his voice, heard from the hallway before he entered the bar, and from his face when he appeared, it was plain that no such stroke of luck had come his way and, moreover, that he had been drinking to console himself.

He stared at Tom for a moment as if he did not recognize him and then barked: 'What the hell are you doing here?'

'Waiting for you, sir,' Tom replied.

'Skiving off, eh? Things got a bit too hot for you out there?'

'No!'

'Got yourself cashiered, is that it? Conduct unbecoming? Well, it's no good coming to me to bail you out.'

'No,' Tom said, trying to keep his voice level, 'that's not why I'm here. I'm on leave, quite legitimately, and I've been made aware that there are things at home that require your attention. I want you to come home with me.'

'Been made aware, have you?' his father repeated satirically. 'Aware of what, may I ask?'

'Certain financial matters.'

'Financial matters? You insolent puppy! What do you know about my financial matters?'

'I know,' Tom said, lowering his voice, 'that if something is not done soon you and mother may be turned out of the house.'

'Turned out! *Turned out!* How dare you come here and make threats like that to me? I know what it is. You're worried about your inheritance! Well, let me tell you this. You can starve in the gutter for all I care. You and your arty-crafty friends. Don't you come here and tell me how to conduct my life. Now get out, before I take my stick to you!'

His father's face had gone from red to purple and his eyes were bulging, so that Tom found himself wondering if people really did die of apoplexy. His raised voice had drawn disapproving looks and mutters from the other occupants of the bar and at that moment two of the club stewards appeared at his elbows.

'Now then, sir. Let's calm down, shall we? Or we'll have to ask you to leave.'

'Calm down! Calm down! Just let me get at him, the cowardly dog! I'll teach him a lesson he won't forget.'

'Come along, sir. No need for any trouble. The young gentleman didn't mean any harm. Why don't you let us take you up to your room? Time to dress for dinner, isn't it?'

Murmuring similar soothing platitudes the two men manoeuvred Sir George, still muttering threats and curses, out of the room. The club secretary had followed them in and turned to Tom.

'Sorry about that, Lieutenant. But you see our problem.'

'I do indeed,' Tom responded shakily. 'Unfortunately, I have no idea what to do about it.'

'It's not the first time this sort of thing has happened. I'm afraid if it goes on we shall have no alternative but to ask Sir George to leave. The other members won't tolerate that kind of behaviour.'

'I understand,' Tom said. 'You must do as you think fit. I'm afraid if I try to interfere any further it will only make things worse.' Privately, he thought that if his father were to find himself out on the street with nowhere to go but home to Denham it might bring him to his senses.

Out in the street himself he was at a loss where to go next. He had no appetite for dinner, and the prospect of returning to the gloom of Denham Hall was too depressing to contemplate. Then he remembered something he had intended to do while in London, before all his plans fell apart. He hailed a cab and set out for Sussex Gardens.

When Beavis opened the door to him he said, 'I've come to enquire if you have any news of Miss Malham Brown? I haven't heard from her for months.'

'Miss Leonora is in the drawing room, sir. Shall I tell her you are here?'

'Leo, here? That's marvellous! Don't worry, Beavis. I'll announce myself.'

Tom bounded into the drawing room and stopped short at the sight of Leo reclining on a chaise longue, pale-faced and *en déshabillé*.

She started up at his entry and gave a small cry. 'Tom! Oh, Tom, how wonderful! I'm so glad to see you.'

He crossed to her side and knelt by the chaise. 'Leo, you're not well. What is it? What has happened? I thought you were in Salonika.'

She sank back against the cushions. 'Oh, I left there some time ago. So much has happened since. I don't know how to tell you . . .'

'Tell me what?'

'Sasha is dead.'

He caught her hand. 'Oh, my dear. I am so sorry.'

'That is not all.'

'What else? Tell me, please!'

He listened in growing anguish as Leo related the events of the past year: the culmination of her love affair with Sasha; her pregnancy; their final encounter; her dash to be at his side when he was wounded; her prolonged labour; the birth of her daughter and how the child had been left in the care of a stranger, and her desperate attempt to return to the village.

'It was a stupid thing to do. I nearly died and the next thing I knew I was on a ship back to England. And now the village is back in Bulgarian hands and I'm stuck here like a helpless invalid.'

He raised her hand to his cheek. 'My dear girl! What can I say? I am so sorry for you. I know how much you loved Sasha, and how it hurt you when he had to marry someone else.'

'But that marriage was never consummated,' she said quickly. 'He swore that. I had a letter from him, Tom, written just before he was killed. In it he told me that he had repudiated his marriage to Eudoxie and made my child, our child, his heir. But what use is that, when I don't know where she is?'

'We will find her,' Tom said firmly. 'When the war is over, we will go back and find the family who took her in and bring her home.'

'When the war is over . . .' Leo said with a sigh. 'Is it ever going to end, Tom?'

'Of course it is. The Germans must be nearly at the end of their resources. And now the Americans are with us, it can't go on much longer. By the end of the summer you may be reunited with your baby.' He hesitated, then went on: 'But have you thought what it will mean, bringing up a child as an unmarried woman?'

She lifted her chin. 'What do I care? Do you suppose I shall be the only woman in that position after this terrible carnage?'

'Of course,' he said. 'I should have known you better. But bear this in mind: if you want me, I will stand by you. After all, we are still officially engaged.'

She looked at him with a flicker of her old humour. 'So we are. It seems a very long time ago that we agreed to it, but I suppose that doesn't make any difference in the eyes of other people.' She reached out and touched his arm. 'Dear Tom. Thank you. If I were going to settle down with anyone, it would have to be you. I'm so glad you're here. You are the only person I can talk to about Sasha. The only one who understands. After all, you knew him at Adrianople, and later in Belgrade, and I think you fell under his spell a little bit yourself. Aren't I right?'

He smiled. 'Yes, it's true. It was impossible to be indifferent to Sasha Malkovic. "Under his spell". Yes, I think that's right. He had a kind of magic that drew people to him.'

She put her arms round his neck. 'You see? You understand. It's such a relief to talk to you.' Then, drawing back a little: 'But I'm being very selfish. I haven't asked you how you are. You're not wounded. You look surprisingly fit. You're just on routine leave, then?'

'Not exactly,' he said ruefully. 'I've got a bit of a tale to tell, too.'

When he finished she looked at him sombrely. 'Now it's my turn to say I'm sorry. How horrible for you! First losing all your pictures and now this dreadful business with your father.'

'Well, the pictures aren't such a tragedy,' he said. 'I thought it was at first, but after all, I can still paint and I have my original sketch books. Maybe one day I'll paint a new set of pictures, not the same but drawing on the same material. It's just a pity that I've missed the chance of a major showing in a reputable gallery.'

'It will come again,' Leo said firmly. 'Talent like yours has to be recognized eventually. But what are you going to do about your father . . .'

Beavis came in. 'Excuse me, madam. Cook wants to know whether you feel you can eat a little dinner.'

Leo looked at Tom. 'Have you eaten, Tom?'

'No, I haven't, as it happens.'

'I've had no appetite, but tonight I think I could eat something. Ask cook if she can manage dinner for two, Beavis.'

He smiled gravely and Tom saw relief in his face. 'I'm sure she can, madam.'

'And make up a room for Lieutenant Devenish, please. You will stay the night, Tom?'

'To the scandal of the neighbourhood?' he queried, with a grin.

'Who cares? After all, as you reminded me, we are officially engaged.'

At breakfast the next day Tom was pleased to see Leo fully dressed and with a little more colour in her cheeks. As he passed him in the hall, Beavis murmured, 'If I may say so, sir, it's a great comfort to Cook and myself to see you here. Miss Leonora has been so down, so unlike herself, that we've been very worried. Nothing seemed to cheer her. But your arrival has really perked her up.'

As they ate Tom asked, 'Are you all on your own, Leo? Aren't there any friends who could keep you company?'

'Oh, yes,' she replied. 'Victoria is in London. Poor girl! She's had a bad time, too. Her lorry overturned and left her trapped under it in a ditch full of freezing water. She's had a broken leg and double pneumonia. She's getting over it, but it's been a long haul and she's been pretty fed up. We've been sharing our misery!'

'Well, perhaps you can start to share your recovery now,' Tom suggested.

Leo gave him a bleak look. 'Easier said than done, old chap. But don't you worry about me. You've got your own problems to sort out. Are you going home today?'

'I must. I'd much rather stay here with you, but something has to be done about Denham. Though God knows what!'

When Tom descended from the trap outside his front door an hour or two later it was immediately flung open by Lowndes, grey-faced and wild-haired.

'Oh, Mr Tom! Thank God you're here! Terrible news! Terrible!'

'What? What's happened? Pull yourself together, man. What's wrong?'

'It's Sir George, sir . . . your father. He's dead.'

'Dead? How? When?'

'A policeman called an hour ago, sir. He's in the morning room, with Mr Standing. I sent word to Mr Standing, sir, in your absence. I didn't know what else to do. Her Ladyship has shut herself in her room and refuses to speak to anyone.'

Tom strode past the butler and into the morning room. Standing and a man in the uniform of a police inspector rose to their feet as he entered.

'What's going on?' Tom demanded. 'What has happened?'

'It's your father, sir,' the inspector said. 'The servants at his club found him in his room this morning. He had put the barrel of his revolver into his mouth and pulled the trigger.'

Eleven

Leo threw the newspaper aside and wandered restlessly to the window. Outside the leaves on the trees drooped, parched and dusty in the heat of June. She turned as the door of the room opened and Beavis announced: 'Miss Langford, ma'am.'

Victoria entered, leaning on a walking stick. 'Phew!' she said, pulling off her hat. 'It's scorching out. What have you been doing with yourself?'

'Not much,' Leo answered morosely.

'What is it?' Victoria asked. She propped the stick against a chair and limped over to Leo. 'You look a bit down. Has something happened?'

'Have you seen the papers today?'

'Only to glance at. Why?'

'General Serrail's forces have called off their attempt to break out of the Salonika salient.' Leo shook her head wearily. 'When we read that there was a new campaign I felt sure that this time they would succeed and before long they would be marching into Serbia. But now it seems we're back where we started.'

'But Bitola is still holding out?'

'By the skin of their teeth, yes. But that doesn't help. Lavci is still in Bulgarian hands.' She put both hands to her temples. 'I can't bear it, Vita! I'm going mad here, thinking about my baby in the middle of all that destruction.'

'It may not be as bad as you imagine,' Victoria said. 'After all, if the Bulgars are in control they won't be shelling the village and if our people have called off the attack they won't, either.'

'But that just means a stalemate, and I'm no nearer being able to go and find her.'

'I know it's hard,' Victoria said gently, 'but you must just try to be patient. The war can't go on much longer and as soon as it's over you will be able to go and collect her.'

'And meanwhile she's learning to call a Serbian peasant woman "mother"!' Leo responded passionately.

'Leo, she's not six months old yet. She won't be calling anyone mother for a long time yet.'

'But she will think of that other woman as her mother. When I finally get to her she won't know me.' Leo sank down on to the sofa and put her head in her hands.

She was surprised by the sudden harshness in Victoria's voice. 'For goodness sake, Leo! Pull yourself together! You're not the only woman in the world to have lost a child, you know. And at least yours is still alive, as far as you know.'

Leo looked up but Victoria's back was turned. She swallowed and wiped her eyes. 'Yes, you're right. I must stop feeling sorry for myself.'

Victoria swung round and sat beside her and Leo saw that her eyes were damp, too. 'No, that was unkind of me. I'm sorry. I can just about imagine what you're going through. But small children forget very quickly, don't they? Once Alexandra's back here she'll soon forget she was ever with that other family.'

Leo jumped up again and paced back to the window. Then she turned to face her friend. 'I'm going back to Salonika.'

'Leo, you can't!' Victoria came to her. 'My dear, you must be sensible! You are not strong enough to withstand the journey. And what would you do if you got there? Sit around, waiting for something to happen? Or start nursing again?'

'Nurse, I suppose.'

'But remember what you told me about conditions out there. Malaria, typhus – and now this new Spanish flu they keep talking about. If you caught something like that you would probably die – and then what would happen to your poor little girl?'

'I suppose she'd grow up as a Serbian peasant and never know the difference,' Leo said despondently.

'I wonder. It's quite possible that the woman who is looking after her will try to be honest with her, and tell her that she isn't her daughter. She might grow up expecting a lady to come and take her back to a wonderful life in England. And if you go and get yourself killed it will never happen.'

Leo gazed at her in horror. 'Vita, that's a terrible thought!'

'So it's important for you to be sensible and stay here until it's safe for you to go back,' Victoria concluded.

Leo returned to the sofa and sank down. 'You're right, of course. But it's hard, Vita. I'm not used to sitting around waiting.'

'I know.' Victoria patted her arm. 'I do understand. But try to be patient. Who knows? By the end of the summer it could all be over.'

Leo looked at her and felt a surge of gratitude. 'I'm so glad you're here, Vita. I know it's an awful thing to say, considering what you had to go through, but your accident has been a blessing in disguise for me.'

Victoria grinned ruefully. 'Well, I didn't see it quite that way at the time. But as things have turned out it was all for the best. I should hate to think of you all on your own here while I was in France.'

'That's what I mean. I don't know how I'd have got through these last months without you to turn to.' Leo put her arm round Victoria's neck. 'You've been such a good friend to me, for all these years.'

'Well, it's mutual.' Victoria blushed and detached herself, and Leo let her go. She knew from long experience that her friend was not given to emotional demonstrations.

The thought released her temporarily from the constant, unremitting cycle of anxiety and frustration which occupied most of her waking moments, and reminded her of something else.

'I had a letter from Luke this morning.'

'Oh, yes?' Victoria's tone was one of studied neutrality. 'I rather thought you had lost touch with him.'

'So did I, until today. One or two of his letters caught up with me in Corfu, telling me about the terrible conditions on Gallipoli and then that he'd been wounded and evacuated to Egypt. But when I moved on to Salonika I suppose we lost contact again, and of course there was no way of getting letters in or out of Bitola, so I thought he'd given up and stopped writing. But then this arrived today, to say he's in France.'

'In France? His wound can't have been too severe, then.'

'Well, I think it was pretty bad at the time. He nearly lost his leg. But now it's all healed and he's been redeployed to the Western Front.'

'Poor man!'

'Yes.' Leo paused, uncertain whether to reveal the next piece of information. Five years had passed since Victoria had ended her affair with Luke but Leo was not sure how she would react. 'That's not the only bit of news.'

'Oh?'

'He's married.'

'Married?' Victoria's face expressed nothing beyond polite interest. 'To a local girl, I suppose.'

'No. You'll never guess who.'

'It can't be anyone we know, surely.'

'Do you remember Sophie?'

'Sophie? The little Serbian nurse at Adrianople? But I thought she was in love with that Greek doctor.'

'Iannis. Yes, she was, and apparently they did marry. According to Luke's letter, he bumped into Sophie when he was on Gallipoli. He doesn't make it clear what he was doing but I get the impression it was some kind of clandestine operation. Anyway, he found out that Iannis had been shot by the Turks, who accused him of being a traitor, and Sophie was left with a small child, a boy . . .' Leo referred to the letter, '. . . Anton, that's it. She was obviously in a dangerous situation so Luke managed to get her back to our lines and she volunteered to help on one of the hospital ships. Then, when he was wounded, she nursed him. He reckons he owes her his life. Anyway, she couldn't go back to Macedonia so Luke decided she ought to come to New Zealand with him, but the only way he could get permission to take her back was if they were married.'

'A marriage of convenience, then,' Victoria said, a little too quickly.

'Well, at first. But this is what he writes . . . Yes, here . . . *Of course it was only a marriage of convenience but on the long voyage back home I suppose we learned to love each other, so when we got back we decided to make a proper go of it. With the result that I now have a baby daughter, Nadia, as well as a stepson. She was born after I left for Cairo so I haven't seen her, but I'm told she has inherited the family red hair. I hope she'll forgive me for that when she grows up! I just pray that I'll survive to see that day.*' Leo folded the letter and looked at her friend.

'Are you OK?'

'Why shouldn't I be?'

'Well, you and he were . . . close, once upon a time.'

'That was years ago.' Victoria sat for a moment with her head turned away. Then she said, 'I hope he'll be very happy. And I hope he gets to see his little girl. I . . . I behaved very badly back then. I've regretted it bitterly since. But I suppose I was very young and naïve. You tried to warn me, but I just thought it was all terribly exciting and . . . and modern. I didn't understand how much I could hurt someone. I'm glad he's found someone . . . someone more worthy of him.'

Leo leaned over and put her hand on her friend's. 'Perhaps you should write to him and tell him that.'

Victoria shook her head. 'I don't suppose he wants to hear from me. You can give him my regards when you write, if you like. Tell him I wish him all the best.'

'I'll do that.'

Victoria got up impatiently. 'What we both need is a breath of fresh air. Come on, get your hat. Now that my leg's strong enough to use the clutch and I've got Sparky back from France I can't wait to get out on the open road. Let's have a run down to Brighton.' Sparky was her pet name for her little yellow Sunbeam car.

'And listen to the guns from across the Channel?' Leo queried grimly.

'All right, then, we'll go the other way. How about a day by the river?'

'I don't really feel like joyriding,' Leo said.

'I don't care what you feel like! It'll do you good to get out of the house. Anyway, I need a change of scene. You're not going to make me go alone, are you?'

Reluctantly, Leo fetched her hat and followed Victoria out to the car. But in the event, the afternoon turned out better than she expected. They drove down to Henley and had tea at a restaurant with lawns that sloped down to the river. The air was cooler than in London, and as they watched young men on leave, poling wives and girlfriends in punts, and school-boys skimming the water in skiffs, it was almost possible to believe that peace had come at last.

In the early hours of the following morning Leo woke with a start. The whole house seemed to shudder and a glass orna-ment on her dressing table tinkled. A split second later she heard a distant rumble. Her first thought was thunder, but that would not have made the house shake. The next possibility that came to mind was an earthquake. She had experienced tremors in Turkey as a child. But in London? Surely not. Was it possible that she had heard the guns firing in France? She knew that it was a constant background sound on the south coast but she had never heard it in London before. She wondered if this meant that some devastating new weapon had been fired. She got out of bed and went to the window. The air was still and heavy but she could not see or hear anything unusual and after a few moments she went back to bed and fell into an uneasy sleep.

Standing to in the first faint light of dawn under the ridge leading up to the village of Messines, Luke was blown against the back of the trench by the explosion – or rather by a rapid series of explosions. Climbing on to the fire-step he saw fountains of earth rising like giant mushrooms all along the ridge. He did not have time to count them, but he reckoned there were a dozen or more.

'What the . . .?' he ejaculated.

'Mines,' said the lieutenant. 'That'll give Fritz a bit of a shake up.'

Then the whistles started blowing and the time for conversation was over. All along the trench men scrambled to the surface and began to charge up the hill towards the village, Luke among the leaders. He had expected to be met with a lethal barrage of machine-gun fire, but instead there were only a few random bursts. As he neared the top men began to emerge from the German trenches and blockhouses, but they made no attempt to fire at the approaching New Zealanders. Instead, stunned and disoriented by the explosions, they raised their hands in surrender and allowed themselves to be rounded up. By seven in the morning, the combined Anzac force was in complete control of Messines.

Luke stood on the crest of the ridge and looked around him. 'Hey, fellers! Look over there.'

His nearest companions crowded round. 'What at? What can you see?'

'Green fields!' Luke said. 'That's the first bit of grass I've seen since we got to this godforsaken place.'

They understood then, and for a few moments they all stood silent, gazing first behind them and then at the view ahead. Behind was a landscape of blackened earth, pockmarked with shell-craters and the broken stumps of trees, the only sign of life the endless columns of men and machinery that crawled across it. Ahead, beyond the German lines, were the undisturbed fields and woods of a gentle rural countryside, mantled with green. It was like looking into Paradise.

It was too easy to last. Soon after midday the Germans counter-attacked. Hunkered down behind the broken wall that was all that remained of one of the village houses, Luke aimed and fired until the barrel of his rifle was red hot. Shells were bursting all around him and the howling sound of the German *minewerfer* mortars, the 'moaning minnies', filled the air. At dusk the enemy gave up the battle and retired, leaving the Anzacs in possession, but looking around him Luke realized that the cost had been very high in terms of casualties. A line of stretcher-bearers was plodding down the hill towards the dressing stations and all around him were the bodies of those who were beyond the help of medicine.

The scream of engines above him made him look up. High above the ridge four planes swooped and twisted. Two bore the black crosses of Germany, the other two the red, white and blue roundels of the Royal Flying Corps. As he watched, one of the German planes spouted black smoke and dived to hit the ground somewhere behind the lines. The other turned tail and disappeared. A cheer went up from the weary men on the ground. They had watched a number of similar encounters over the last weeks and it was apparent to all of them that the RFC had established an unquestionable superiority in the air battle.

Rations were brought up and passed out; camp fires were lit and sentries posted. Luke wrapped himself in his greatcoat and settled down in the lea of a sheltering wall. The guns had stopped and the first stars were showing in the summer night. Somewhere down on the plain a nightingale began to sing.

Tom, bivouacking with his company in a ruined farmhouse on the outskirts of Ypres, was jolted awake by the explosion. He found Ralph standing by what remained of a window embrasure. 'What the hell was that?'

'Mines,' Ralph said. 'Our boys have been tunnelling for months to get right under the Boche positions. Those explosions should have shattered their strong-points all along the ridge. Bloody good show!' He turned to address the sleepy men who were crowding forward. 'OK, lads. Nothing to get excited about. Get some shut-eye while you still have the chance.'

Tom felt no inclination to go back to sleep so he stayed where he was, watching the sky slowly lighten, glad of a few minutes to himself to think. He had rejoined the Second

Battalion when they were still encamped along the Somme, but soon they had received orders to march east, back to the Ypres salient where they had fought all those months before. His duties had given him little time to brood on the events of his last leave, for which he was grateful.

He had to admit to himself that his first emotion on hearing the news of his father's suicide had been relief. Guilt, the nagging thought that he might have precipitated it by his confrontation with him, came later. Initially, he was carried along by the realization that the problems resulting from his father's behaviour were now within his power to address. The estate was entailed, so he was the unquestioned heir and able to act as he saw fit. His leave had been extended by a week, on compassionate grounds, and in that time he was able to arrange for the whole lot to be auctioned and the debts paid off. It would have been possible, just, to retain possession of the house, but he realized that without the farmlands to provide an income it would rapidly become a millstone round his neck, so that went too. His only concern was for his mother, who had withdrawn almost completely into a world of her own, but it was obvious that as long as she had her embroidery it would not matter to her where she lived. There was a house on the estate, the original Dower House, which had been let to a local doctor, but he had been called up and his family had moved to live with the wife's sister, leaving the house empty. It was a pleasant, five-bedroomed Georgian building with its own garden, and this was the only part of his inheritance that Tom decided to retain, for his mother to live in.

Most of the staff were happy to accept the wages that were owing to them and seek other employment. With so many men away at the war, and women earning better wages than ever before in the munitions factories, there was no shortage of vacancies. But Lowndes and Morag, his mother's personal maid who had been with her for years, elected to stay on and move with her to the Dower House. With a girl to come in every day from the village to do the heavy work, Tom could feel satisfied that she would be well looked after.

When everything had been decided, Tom had time to

consider the fact that everything he had grown up with, and had expected one day to inherit, had vanished. Only the title remained and he found it laughable that he should be addressed as Sir Thomas. He felt a passing nostalgia for the woods and pastures he had known as a boy, but his principal emotion was one of relief. He was free of the past, and could make whatever he wished of his future . . . assuming, that was, that he had a future. Standing by the window, listening to the first cocks crowing and the first gunfire of the day starting up, it seemed unlikely.

Yesterday they had marched through Ypres and he had been horrified by what had happened to the city since he had first seen it. The magnificent Gothic Cloth Hall had been reduced to a smouldering ruin and the remaining inhabitants were living like troglodytes in the cellars of their shattered houses. The sight seemed to encapsulate all the futile waste of the last three years. The mood of the men was different, too. They sang as they marched, but the songs were no longer the breezily optimistic melodies of 'It's a Long Way to Tipperary' or 'Pack Up Your Troubles'. Instead they had a note of weary endurance. 'We're here because we're here,' they sang, 'we're here because we're here.'

Tom sighed and looked at his watch. Time to rouse the men. Time for another long march towards the battle front.

Twelve

All through the long, hot days of June and into July Tom and his men trained and rehearsed every conceivable manoeuvre in trench warfare. The trench system stretched back from the front line to a depth of eight miles and had taken on the character of a small town. Every trench or recognizable feature had a name: Piccadilly Circus, Clapham Junction, or the notorious Hellfire Corner. Every day more equipment arrived, more men, more guns, more ammunition. In the mess every evening the same questions were being asked: when are we going to attack? What are the generals waiting for? Morale was high and everyone was convinced that when the attack finally came they would sweep the Germans off the surrounding ridges and push them back to their own borders. The primary objective was Roulers, an important road junction, but the ultimate goal was Zeebrugge, from where the German submarine fleet was wreaking heavy losses on the merchant ships bringing vital food to Britain.

'This bloody waiting is getting me down!' Ralph confided in a quiet moment. 'Look at this weather. It's perfect. The ground has dried out, to a large extent, but if it rains – my God, if it rains we'll be bogged down for the rest of the winter.'

'Makes you think that fellow Sassoon has got a point, when he says that the people running the war are incompetent and have no conception of what the fighting men are going through.'

'That bloody conchie!' Ralph turned to stare at Tom. 'Don't tell me you agree with him.'

'No. Not to the extent of refusing to carry on the fight. But I do think his letter to *The Times* raised some important points. Haven't you, secretly, had some of the same thoughts yourself? Be honest.'

'Well,' Ralph agreed grudgingly, 'he's not wrong when he says that people back home don't know what it's like out here, and don't care much either. But I still believe this is a war we had to fight, and one we have to win. I just wish the brass hats would let us get on with it.'

Finally, at the end of July, the orders came through to prepare for an all-out attack. On the night of July the thirtieth the artillery began a creeping barrage, designed to move forward at a predetermined rate so that the infantry could follow it. Once again, Tom found himself standing to in a forward trench, waiting for the whistles to blow. A few feet away, Ralph stood with his eyes glued to his watch. Zero hour was timed for 3.50 a.m., an hour before dawn.

The noise of the guns subsided for a moment as the gunners adjusted their aim, and then the whistles blew and Tom hauled himself up the ladder and out into no-man's-land. He saw

Ralph running ahead of him, waving the men to follow, and plunged forward. Whizzbangs and moaning minnies howled over his head, but he was so used to the noise that he scarcely heard them. Ahead the ground was pitted with shell-holes created by their own artillery, but the German trenches remained strangely quiet. Before he expected it, they were in among them. A scrawny lad appeared in front of Tom and held up his hands in abject surrender. Tom grabbed him, took his rifle and gave him a shove. 'Go! Get out of it! Back there.' The boy understood the gesture if not the words and trotted off towards the British lines, where Tom knew there were people who would be only too ready to take him prisoner. As he ran on the skeletal remains of trees appeared out of the mist and he recognized it as one of the objectives he had studied on his map. This must be Artillery Wood.

Close by he saw the remains of a German blockhouse and suddenly a machine gun opened up from inside it. Ralph shouted an order and Tom waved the three nearest men to follow him. He saw Ralph lob a grenade into the blockhouse and heard the explosion. Moments later two boys staggered out, with their hands in the air. When they had been disarmed and dispatched Tom and Ralph and their small group stood panting in the lee of the building.

'It's too easy!' Ralph said. 'Where are they?'

'They're just kids,' Tom responded. 'The Germans have put them here as cannon fodder. My guess is they are keeping their best troops back, out of harm's way.'

'Bastards!' Ralph muttered.

A machine gun opened up from the cover of the trees. It was fully light now and they could make out the position of the sandbagged emplacement where the gunman was sheltering.

'You've always been good at throwing the cricket ball, Tom,' Ralph said. 'See if you can put that swine out of action.'

Tom dropped to the ground and wormed his way forwards until he reckoned he was within throwing range. Then he took a deep breath, jumped to his feet and in the same movement drew back his arm and bowled. The Mills bomb described a perfect trajectory and dropped into the dugout.

The resulting explosion silenced the machine gun and the gunner.

By mid-morning the Coldstreamers had consolidated their positions around the wood and dug in to await reinforcements. Their part of the attack had been a complete success.

Then the rain started. A spatter of droplets first, then a steady drizzle which developed into a torrential downpour. Soon they were all soaked to the skin and the ground, which had been firm when they attacked, became a sea of mud. Behind them, the low ground, which had always been marshy, turned into a quagmire. In the afternoon the German counter-attack began. Shells fell all round, throwing up great gouts of wet earth. Figures appeared out of the murkiness, rifles at the ready. These were not the half-starved youths they had encountered earlier; these were crack German troops. Grimly the Coldstreamers hunkered down and returned fire. The familiar shout began to go up. 'Stretcher-bearers!' but before long a runner came up and panted, 'It's no good, sir. The stretcher-bearers can't get through. Three teams have bogged down in the mud already.' At length, as daylight faded, the line of attackers wavered and retired.

For two days they held out, under continuous rain and equally unrelenting bombardment. Rations ran out on the first day; by the second ammunition was getting very short as well, but they were cut off from all relief by an impassable swamp two miles wide between their position and their own front line. On the third day orders came through that they were to retire. A duckboard pathway had been hastily laid across the morass and slowly, in single file, carrying their wounded, they limped back to base.

Day after day the rain continued. Shellfire had breeched the dykes that had once drained the low-lying Flanders fields. Shell-craters filled with water and joined lip-to-lip to form small lakes. Between them, the mud grew deeper and more liquid. Teams of Pioneers worked under cover of darkness to build roads and paths over it but with daylight the enemy gunners found the tracks easy targets and the work had to be done again and again. Horses slipped off the paths and sank up to their hocks in the mud. Sometimes the riders were trapped beneath them and it required more men and horses to drag them free. Usually the horse had to be shot. Sweating, cursing men hauled on ropes to pull carts and gun carriages out of the swamp. But somehow the roads were built and on August the ninth the rain stopped at last.

Once again Tom led his men into the attack. Once again they penetrated the German front line, only to be held by a heavily fortified line of blockhouses and machine-gun nests. Then the Germans began to lay down a barrage behind them, making retreat or reinforcement equally impossible. Once more they were cut off from food, water and fresh supplies of ammunition. Men stood for hours at a time up to their knees in mud and water, while the shells dropped around them. The stagnant water in the craters was polluted by dead bodies of friend and foe alike. Undrinkable, it was even too filthy to be used to wash away the mud. When they were finally relieved Tom reckoned he had been without food or sleep for three days and nights. Nevertheless, once they were back in the reserve trenches he felt it was his duty to ensure that his men were looked after, as far as it was possible in the dank dugouts. He was examining the feet of one of them for signs of trench foot when Ralph's orderly appeared at his elbow.

'Excuse me, sir. Major Malham Brown asks you to take this note back to Major Ransome at Battalion HQ.'

Tom got to his feet and took the envelope. The last thing he wanted at that moment was a long trudge through the communications trench back to HQ, and he wondered through the mists of exhaustion why Ralph could not have sent a runner with the message. However, orders were orders and presumably the message was too vital to be entrusted to an ordinary soldier. He slapped the shoulder of the man he had been examining and said, 'OK, Jonesy. You'll do,' and set off.

HQ was situated in the cellars of a ruined house. By the time he reached it Tom was swaying on his feet. Ransome took the letter, read it and nodded. Then he looked at Tom. 'You look just about ready to drop, old man. Get some sleep.'

'No.' Tom shook his head blearily. 'Got to get back . . .'

'What you have got to do,' said Ransome, quite pleasantly, 'is what you're damn well told. There's a bed through there.' He indicated an adjoining cellar. 'Get your head down.'

Tom staggered into the cellar, threw himself down fully clothed on a camp bed and slept for twenty-four hours.

When he finally stumbled, blinking, into the lamplight of the following evening, Ransome was just sitting down to eat. He looked Tom over and remarked, 'That's better. A wash and brush up and a decent meal and you might look half human. Here, have a drink.'

He poured Tom a glass of whisky and continued as he drank it: 'Do you know what was in that letter you brought?'

Tom shook his head. 'No idea, sir.'

Ransome fished the letter out of his pocket and handed it to Tom. It read: *Devenish is just about done in. Please put him to bed.*

Thirteen

In the dog days of August Leo had finally found a project to stir her out of her lethargy. It came to her when she was packing up a parcel of small luxuries to send to Ralph and Tom. As she wrapped a tin of cherry jam she remembered how much the Serbian soldiers she had known loved jam and how poorly fed and clothed they were. The ordinary soldiers came mostly from poor peasant families, who found it hard enough to feed those at home without sending much-needed provisions to their sons in the trenches. There were no committees of well-meaning ladies knitting socks and mufflers for them and no Red Cross parcels. They survived on the bare necessities and sometimes lacked even those. Immediately, she knew what she must do. She must somehow raise funds to provide a few small comforts for the men she had lived and worked with so closely.

She began by seeking the advice of her father's old friend

at the Foreign Office. He listened to the story of her experiences, suitably edited to omit all references to Sasha and the
lost child, and then exclaimed: 'My dear girl! People will be
fascinated to hear about all this. What you must do is hire a
hall and advertise in the papers that you are going to give a
lecture about them – you know the kind of thing. "An English
lady with the Serbian Army". Invite a few influential people
– I can give you some names and I'm sure you can think of
others – and start a subscription. I guarantee that in a couple
of months you will have enough money to send any amount
of jam, and anything else you think might be appreciated.'

'You want me to stand up in front of a hall full of people
and talk?' Leo said doubtfully.

He leaned back in his chair and raised his eyebrows. 'Are
you trying to tell me, after everything you've done, that you
are frightened of speaking to a civilized English audience?'

Leo took a deep breath. 'No, you're right. Anyway, it's the
least I can do.'

By the end of the month she had found a hall and placed
the advertisements in four daily papers. Initially there seemed
to be little interest. The fighting on the Western Front was of
far more immediate concern to people in England. The Serb's
heroic retreat had been consigned to a distant memory and
the Salonika front was referred to only in the context of musical
hall jokes suggesting that it was a good place for skivers who
wanted to avoid the fighting. Then something happened to
bring it to the forefront of people's minds. Leo was stunned
to open her paper one morning and read that a devastating
fire had swept through the city, destroying most of the old
buildings. She sat for a long time, remembering the vision of
the city rising out of the mists as she sailed towards it, with
its towers and minarets. She thought of the *caravanserai* where
she and Victoria had slept that first night, and the narrow
streets where they had been accosted by the drunken soldiers.
She remembered the Makedonia Palace Hotel, where she had
first seen Sasha, Floca's, where they had spent so many happy
evenings, and above all the room in the small pension where
they had slept together. She wondered if her friends at the
Red Cross hospital were safe, and the British and French

officers whom she had known during that last summer. In spite of her worries, she had to admit that the fire had done one good thing, at least. Salonika was back in the public mind and she was determined to use that to the best advantage.

She was busy writing letters to everyone she could think of who might help with her fund-raising efforts when Beavis came into the room.

'Pardon me, madam. There's a man at the door, a sergeant in the New Zealand army. He says his name is Luke Pavel and he claims to be an old friend.'

'Luke!' Leo jumped to her feet. 'Show him in at once, Beavis.'

'Very good, madam.' The butler retreated, his back stiff with disapproval at the idea of admitting a non-commissioned officer, and a colonial to boot.

When Luke entered the room Leo was shocked by how much he had changed. He was no longer the romantic boy with the ready grin she had known at Lozengrad and Adrianople. This was a man whose weather-beaten face was lined with exhaustion and whose eyes were shadowed with bitter experience.

She recovered herself quickly and went to take his hand. 'Luke, this is a wonderful surprise. I'm delighted to see you.'

'I hope you don't mind,' he said awkwardly. 'I wasn't sure until this morning that I'd actually get to London, so I didn't write to tell you I was coming. I thought I'd call in on the off chance. I guess that's not the way things are done over here.'

'Oh, nonsense!' she exclaimed. 'You don't have to stand on ceremony. You're on leave, of course. Not wounded, I hope?'

'No. I'm all in one piece – so far, anyway.'

'That's good to know. Come and sit down. You will stay for luncheon, won't you?'

'If that's not too much trouble. It's a bit short notice.'

'Not at all. Of course you must stay.' Leo rang the bell. 'Now, tell me all your news. Is it terrible in France?'

'Pretty bad.'

'Not worse than Gallipoli, surely. From your letters that sounded like hell on earth.'

'Near enough. But Flanders runs it close. It comes down

to the question of whether you'd rather burn or drown, I guess.'

'You poor man!' Beavis came in and Leo said, 'Sergeant Pavel is staying to lunch, Beavis. And I'm sure he would like a drink beforehand. I'm going to have sherry, Luke, but I expect you'd rather have something stronger. Whisky and soda?'

'That would be great.'

'Thank you, Beavis.'

'Very good, madam.'

When the butler had gone Leo went on: 'I read in the papers that you Anzacs distinguished yourselves at Messines. Well done! Was it a very hard fight?'

'Not to start with. But we lost a lot of men in the German counter-attack. Then a day or two later we were ordered to push on to a place called La Basseville, across the River Lys. That was tough going. We won it and lost it and won it back again over the course of two or three days. Then we were relieved and I was lucky enough to get leave.'

'How long have you got?'

'It was a week, but I spent the first two days getting here. Men going on leave don't have a high priority when it comes to seats in railway carriages.'

Beavis re-entered carrying a tray. 'Your drinks, madam. And Miss Langford is in the hall.'

'Oh, God!' Leo clapped her hand over her mouth to stifle the exclamation. She had completely forgotten that she had invited Victoria for lunch. Before she could speak, Victoria was in the room, handing her walking stick to the butler.

'Take this horrible thing away and hide it, Beavis! I'm determined to learn to do without it.' Then, turning to Leo: 'I'm sorry. I didn't realize you had a visitor.' She stopped short, staring. 'Luke? It is you, isn't it? Leo, why didn't you tell me . . .?'

Luke broke in. 'I just looked in on the off chance. I didn't know . . . Look, I'm going to be in the way. I'll go.'

'You will do nothing of the sort!' Leo said robustly. 'Vita, Luke's just come back from the fighting in Flanders. I've invited him to lunch.'

'Of course.' Victoria recovered herself. 'Please don't go on my account, Luke.' She crossed to him and held out her hand. 'How do you do?'

'I'm fine, thanks,' Luke responded, flushed with confusion. 'But how about you? I mean, why the walking stick?'

'I had a bit of an accident last January – skidded into a ditch. Careless of me.'

He grinned suddenly. 'You always were a tiger behind the wheel of a car.'

'It wasn't a car,' Leo said. 'It was an ambulance and poor Vita was trapped under it for hours, up to her neck in freezing water.'

'Jeez! I'm sorry. I didn't mean to make light of it . . .' Luke's confusion was increasing.

'I'd much rather you did,' Victoria said. 'It really wasn't anything to make a fuss about.'

Beavis was hovering with the tray of drinks. Leo said, 'Will you have a sherry before luncheon, Vita? I'm having one.'

Victoria looked at the tray. 'I think I'll have something stronger, to celebrate Luke's arrival. Bring me a horse's neck, please, Beavis.'

Beavis's face took on a martyred expression. He disapproved of the new fashion for cocktails, especially when drunk by young women. 'Very good, madam,' he said on a sigh and left the room.

'Do sit down, both of you,' Leo said.

They sat and for a moment nobody spoke. Leo was trying to work out how to deal with the situation. Victoria had been very non-committal when she had shown her Luke's letter and she could not guess what her friend's feelings towards him were, after a lapse of so many years.

Luke broke the silence. 'Look, Leo, I didn't mean to gate-crash. I mean, I'm not used to moving in these aristocratic surroundings . . .'

Leo looked round the room and was aware for the first time in years of the ornate chandeliers and the overstuffed furniture.

'Oh, there's nothing "aristocratic" about this place. This was my grandmother's house. It's badly in need of redecorating and refurnishing, to get rid of all this stuffy Victoriana. But I've had other things on my mind. And don't get the wrong idea. My grandfather was a self-made man who got his money building railways.'

Beavis returned with Victoria's drink, then turned to Leo. 'Pardon me, madam, but cook would like a word with you.'

Leo could guess what the problem was. She excused herself to her guests and made her way down to the kitchen, where she found the cook glowering at two small lamb chops.

'This was all I could get from the butcher this morning, Miss Leo, and the boy had to stand in a queue for an hour to get these. And now you ask an extra gentleman to lunch. You tell me how I'm supposed to make three meals out of two chops.'

Leo laid a hand on her arm. 'I'm sorry. You look after me so well it's easy to forget for a moment how difficult things are. But the problem is easy to solve. Give both the chops to Sergeant Pavel and Miss Langford and I will make do with vegetables. I'll tell him we're on a special diet.'

Back in the drawing room she sensed an atmosphere of understandable constraint. She lifted her glass of sherry. 'Sorry about that. Cheers!'

Victoria took her cue and raised her glass in turn. 'Welcome to London, Luke! Oh, and I've just remembered, congratulations! Leo told me you are married. How is Sophie?'

Luke lowered his glass, untouched, his face suddenly bereft of expression.

Leo leaned towards him. 'Luke? What is it? What's wrong?'

He spoke as if dragging the words from deep within him. 'I wasn't going to mention this till later. Sophie died. I heard last week.'

'Sophie, dead?' For a moment Leo could think of nothing else to say. Was there to be no end to the death and destruction, even in a remote corner of the earth like New Zealand?

'It was some sort of flu,' he said, his tone flat. 'She volunteered to help in the hospital in Wellington. They reckon it came in with one of the hospital ships coming back from Europe. They say it was all over very quickly.'

Leo looked at Victoria, who sat like a graven image. She

got up and went to crouch beside Luke's chair. 'My dear, I am so sorry. To think she survived the typhus and all the other horrors in Adrianople, only to be struck down just when she seemed to have found a safe place. You must be devastated.'

He looked at her, and his expression was hurt and puzzled, like a child unfairly punished. He said, 'It's strange. We were married for such a short time. Only a few months. And I've been away now for almost a year. It's sort of . . . unreal. It's hard to believe it ever happened.'

'What about your little girl?' Leo said gently. 'Is she all right?'

'Oh, yes. She's being looked after by my mother. I've got a photograph.'

He fumbled for his wallet and produced a blurred image of a chubby child. The sight tore at Leo's heart strings. 'She'll be waiting for you when you get home, Luke,' she said huskily. 'You have that to look forward to, at least.'

He nodded numbly. 'And Anton – Sophie's boy. Funny to think I've got a ready-made family waiting for me.'

'Be grateful for that,' Leo said, and turned away.

Beavis appeared at that moment to announce that luncheon was served. Victoria regarded her meatless plate with a puzzled frown and Leo said breezily, 'Vita and I have given up meat for the moment. It's the latest health advice. And I'm sure we feel better for it, don't we, Vita?'

'Oh, yes,' Victoria mumbled. 'Definitely.'

It was not an easy meal. Leo was haunted by the little-boy-lost look in Luke's eyes and could think of no way of banishing it, while Victoria remained unusually taciturn. Leo managed to keep the conversation going on neutral topics, mainly to do with the news from the battle front, but it was clear that Luke had no desire to be reminded of conditions out there. She racked her brains for some way to distract him. Finally, with the coffee, she said, 'Vita, we should do something to entertain Luke while he's on leave. Why don't we take him to the Coliseum?'

'The music hall?' Victoria queried. 'Do you think that's quite . . .?'

'It's not the usual sort of programme,' Leo said. 'They are

giving this new work by Sir Edward Elgar. It's called Fringes of the Fleet, and the words are settings of poems by Rudyard Kipling. I'm told it's very good.'

'Kipling?' Luke said. 'I like his stuff. Let's go.'

For the next few days Leo put aside her fund-raising efforts in order to show Luke round London, and found in the process that she was seeing the city through new eyes. It gave her pleasure to see his unaffected admiration for the splendours of St Paul's and Westminster Abbey, but he was shocked to discover ruined houses, the result of bombs dropped from Zeppelins earlier in the war.

'I'm glad we didn't have to contend with them as well as everything else at Adrianople,' Luke remarked.

'We had our share of them in Calais,' Victoria said, 'until our chaps discovered incendiary bullets. Wow! You should have seen one of them go up!'

Leo had not pressed her to join them but she seemed to take it for granted and it quickly became clear that Luke enjoyed her company. It seemed that the old spark of mutual attraction was not dead. On the last night of Luke's leave they went to dinner at the Savoy and afterwards Leo found that the cab driver had been instructed to drop her off at Sussex Gardens first, leaving him alone with Victoria. Who had arranged it, she was not sure, but she speculated as she undressed for bed that it was not simple coincidence.

Next morning they went to see Luke off at Victoria Station and she watched them both carefully, but their behaviour gave nothing away. After the train had pulled out, however, amid a frenzy of shouts and waves and tears, she was not entirely surprised to see her friend surreptitiously wiping her cheeks.

Fourteen

Tom had come to the conclusion that, if the Somme repre-
sented Dante's Seventh Circle of hell, with its plain of fire,
Ypres in October, with its unending cold and mud, was the
last and lowest circle. All through September the weather had
been fine and the sodden ground had dried out again. That
had allowed new roads to be laid across the swamp. They were
constructed of planks of wood placed side by side and were
quickly nicknamed 'corduroy roads'. The German shelling
continued unabated and very soon these roads were lined with
the bodies of dead mules and overturned wagons, but slowly
the necessary supplies and ammunition were brought
forward to support the new advance. Once again, all had
gone well to start with, in spite of the fact that on the dry
ground the troops were blinded by the dust raised by the
shelling. The Anzac forces took and held the Gravenstal spur
and pushed forwards to the edge of the salient. And then the
rain started again.

By the time Tom and his company were ordered forward
no-man's-land was once again an impassable morass, except
for the narrow duckboard tracks that wandered this way and
that across it. To add to the misery, the Germans had
deployed a new weapon. At first it had stolen up on them
without being noticed, an almost odourless miasma creeping
along the ground, until men's eyes began to sting and they
started to retch and cough. It burnt through the soles of
boots and blistered skin and clung to clothes so that a man
who had been exposed to it could kill the comrades he
shared a dugout with simply by proximity. It was some time
before the British chemists could work out what it was. It
was called mustard gas.

This new hazard meant that as they were deployed the order
went out: 'Gas masks on!' The heavy masks had an eyepiece
of thick, greenish glass which made everything appear as if

seen through water, and which very quickly misted up from the wearer's breath. To negotiate the narrow paths while sight was so restricted was fraught with danger. One false step could send a man sliding into the mud, and once in there was no hope of rescue. Men and even horses disappeared without trace within minutes. Tom, like many of his men, found that prospect more terrifying than the constant shelling.

On October the twelfth the second battalion of the Coldstream Guards was ordered to attack the Bellevue spur, east of Poelcappelle. They went forward behind a creeping barrage, which had proved successful in destroying German resistance on previous occasions. This time it did not seem to be having the same effect. Tom could hear the shells going over his head, but there seemed to be comparatively few explosions.

'I reckon they're dropping on to soft ground and just disappearing into the mud without exploding,' his sergeant remarked grimly.

It was a two and a half mile trudge from the reserve lines to the forward trenches, encumbered with gas masks and other impedimenta. When Tom looked at his men, burdened with extra rations and ammunition, waterproof sheets, entrenching tools, grenades, rifles and their personal kit, he thought it was a wonder that some of them could walk at all. By the time they reached the front line they were all weary; but after a brief respite the whistles blew and they were off again, over the top and into no-man's-land. The ground was firmer here on the ridge, though peppered with shell-holes, and they moved forward in open order, each man a few yards to the right or left of the next. Tom could see Ralph a little ahead and away to his left were the advancing lines of the next battalion. To his right were the men of the Sixty-Sixth Anzacs, newly arrived in Flanders, who were supposed to be guarding the flank.

To begin with they met with little opposition. A few whizz-bangs exploded in front and behind them and there was the occasional zip and ping of a sniper's bullet and a man fell, but there was not the wholesale slaughter Tom remembered from the Somme. Then, unexpectedly, they found themselves facing the German wire, still largely intact in spite of the barrage.

'Spread out!' Ralph ordered. 'Look for a gap.'

There was a frantic scuttle along the line of the wire and then a shout of 'Over here!' They all ran towards the man who had shouted and found a small break in the barbed wire, close to a stream called the Steenbeck. It was wide enough for three men at a time to pass through but as they scrambled forward a machine gun somewhere near the stream opened up. Tom flung himself flat behind the dubious shelter of some scrubby undergrowth and for a while nobody moved. Every time a head was lifted, the gun chattered again. Then he heard Ralph call. 'You two – Robinson, Fletcher – with me. The rest of you keep your heads down.'

Tom peered through the undergrowth and saw Ralph and the other men worming their way forward towards the position of the machine-gun nest. He had to quell the impulse to follow. His place was here, with his men, and Ralph would be relying on that. Moments passed and then he heard a grenade explode, followed by another, and the gun fell silent.

Tom got to his feet. 'Forward, lads! Follow me!'

They ran forward, meeting more fire from a half-demolished pillbox. Tom's sergeant hurled a grenade and the firing stopped. Then men rose up out of the ground ahead of them and it was hand-to-hand, with no time for thought, until suddenly the opposition vanished and they found themselves in possession of the enemy trench. Tom looked around him, panting. There was no sign of Ralph.

Someone shouted, 'Sir! Looks like the Sixty-Sixth are pulling back.'

Tom swung round. It was true that the Anzacs appeared to be retreating. He looked to his other side and could see no sign of the battalion which had been advancing beside them. In the mad dash forward it seemed they had outdistanced the others and held a small salient cut into enemy territory. Tom was well aware of the danger of being cut off and surrounded. He swept one more look around the area and seeing no officer more senior gave the order: 'Pull back!'

They retreated in skirmishing order until they made contact again with the rest of the force, who were digging in under concentrated fire. There was still no sign of Ralph but Tom told himself that in the general confusion he could be anywhere along the line. They started to dig in like the rest but then Tom saw movement ahead among the shattered remnants of trees and a second later a line of grey-clad troops advanced towards them. They were big men, with the look of seasoned campaigners in the way they moved, and they were carrying the most fearsome weapons yet devised – flame-throwers. All along the line the British and Anzac forces opened fire and for a while they held the enemy at bay, but the flame-throwers were too much for some of the men. Tom saw them break ranks and run back, only to be caught on the remains of the wire, where the flame-throwers reduced them to charred corpses in a matter of seconds.

Soon the order came along the line. 'Fall back! Fall back!'

Tom passed the word along the line of his men. 'Fall back in twos, head for the gap we came through. We'll cover you.'

He was the last to make the dash for the gap and once through it found three of his men were missing. To go back to look for them was certain suicide and, to add to his bitter chagrin, in spite of all their efforts, they were back where they had started that morning.

Having checked to see that none of his remaining men was seriously wounded, Tom made his way along the trench, looking for Ralph. Eventually he found Fletcher, one of the men who had gone with him to attack the machine-gun nest, lying on a stretcher with two medics bending over him. He was barely conscious, blood oozing from three bullet wounds in his chest.

Tom leaned close to him. 'Fletcher, where's Major Malham Brown?'

Fletcher mumbled vaguely and Tom repeated his question with greater urgency. 'You were with him. What happened? Did he come back with you?'

The wounded man opened his eyes and Tom sensed that he had recognized him. 'Major's gone, sir. Bastards got him at short range. We fixed them, though. Robbo got them with a Mills bomb.'

A rising tide of panic and despair threatened to overwhelm Tom. 'Where is he?' he repeated. 'You didn't leave him out there, did you?'

But Fletcher had lapsed back into unconsciousness. One of the medics said, 'The major hasn't been brought in, sir. We'd know if he had.'

'What about the other man who was with him? Robinson?'

'Couldn't say, sir. I haven't come across him.'

After a further anguished search Tom found Robinson huddled under a blanket, while another medic dressed a cut on his head.

'Fletcher says the major was shot. Is that true?'

'Yes, sir. We were creeping up close to the machine gun. Then the major stood up to lob a grenade, but the buggers spotted him and gunned him down.'

'Was he killed?'

'No, but it was a bad wound. Fletch and I wanted to bring him back for treatment but he says, "No. You must go on and fix that gun. Don't worry about me". So we did as he said, but then Fletch got his packet. I chucked a grenade into the machine-gun nest. I think I got the lot of them but I threw in a second one to be on the safe side. Then something hit me on the head and knocked me out. I reckon it was a bit of shrapnel from the explosion. Next thing I knew I was on a stretcher being carried back here.'

'So he's still out there – Major Malham Brown?'

'Far as I know, sir.'

Almost unaware of his surroundings, Tom stumbled back along the trench to where his own men were. His first impulse was to organize a rescue-party to go out at once in search of Ralph, but when he stood on the firing step to reconnoitre the ground a sniper's bullet whistled past his ear. The enemy had not pressed home their counter-attack but it was clear that they were in control of the ground beyond the barbed wire and any rescue attempt in daylight was doomed to failure. He stooped to enter the dugout where his men were sheltering. 'Major Malham Brown is out there somewhere, badly wounded. I want three volunteers to come with me as soon as it's dark enough to bring him in.'

A dozen hands went up. Ralph was a popular officer and Tom knew that he, too, was well regarded. He chose the three strongest, recognizing that to bring a wounded man back over that terrain without exposing themselves to the enemy would not be an easy task. For the next hour he stood in the trench, peering through a periscope at the ground in front of him, hoping for some sign of movement and waiting for darkness. A rat ran over his feet but he barely noticed it.

At some point his orderly appeared at his side with a steaming mess tin. 'Brought you a brew, sir. Look as though you could do with it.'

Tom thanked him and swallowed the sweet, scalding liquid almost without tasting it. Then he resumed his vigil. Towards dusk, the rain clouds that had threatened all day cleared, and an almost full moon rose in the sky. The sight reduced Tom to impotent fury and he swore at it in terms he would have despised in calmer moments.

When it was fully dark he called the three volunteers to him. 'You remember where the machine gun was, near the stream? The major is somewhere close to that. We'll leave here in single file. I'll go first, then you, Jamieson, then Williams, then Drew. Once we're through the wire we'll spread out, but stay where we can see each other. In this moonlight it shouldn't be a problem but keep your heads down. Jerry will be able to see just as well as we can. Here's a torch each. If you find the major, signal by two short flashes, then move away from that position in case an enemy sniper has spotted you. Once we have all joined up again, whoever has found him can show us where he is. Understood?'

They nodded and he went on: 'Jamieson, you're the biggest. There's a folding stretcher here. Can you manage to drag that with you?'

'Nae problem, sir,' the Scotsman assured him.

Tom took a final scan through the periscope, then hauled himself over the parapet and began to squirm towards the barbed wire, not on hands and knees but flat on his stomach like a snake, dragging himself forward with his elbows. A glance behind showed him that the other three were all out of the trench and following. The distance to the gap in the wire seemed endless and he was tempted more than once to speed his progress by getting up, but he knew that would be making a target of himself. Once through the gap, he waited for the others to catch him up and waved them to spread out on either side. At that moment, to his relief, the moon went behind a cloud. It was a mixed blessing. Although it made it less likely that they would be spotted, it also meant that it was harder to see the ground ahead and the hundreds of shell-craters made the search almost impossible. Twice Tom almost pitched head first into one, and each one had to be investigated. Several contained bodies, lying half submerged in mud and water, almost unrecognizable. Some Tom ignored because their bloated condition told him they had been dead for days, if not weeks. Others he had to drag over until he could see the face or recognize the badges of rank. Once he pulled at an arm only to have it come away in his hand, almost choking him with the stench of decomposition. He crawled on and on, oblivious of time, resting every now and then when his aching arms would drag him no further.

At last he heard a faint call from his left and turned to see the rapid glimmer of a torch. Instantly there was the crack of a rifle. Skittering crablike across the mud he reached Drew, to find him lying with a neat bullet-hole in the centre of his forehead.

'Bugger you!' he muttered under his breath. 'You and your sniper's rifle. You're too damn good.'

He lifted his head and gazed around him. Ralph was here somewhere. Drew had found him and paid the price.

'Ralph,' he called softly. 'Ralph! It's me. Where are you?'

For a second there was no response, then faintly from nearby he heard a voice. 'Tom? Get back, you bloody fool.'

It came from the bottom of a crater a few feet away and at the sound all Tom's caution vanished. He hurled himself forward until he crouched on the edge. Below him he could see Ralph, lying half-in, half-out of a filthy pool.

'Hold on, old man!' Tom gasped. 'We're going to get you out of there.'

He turned to look for the other two men, who should be closing up on him, but there was no sign of them. He grabbed his torch and flashed it twice, then turned to scramble down to where Ralph lay. As he did so, something hit him in the back like a kick from a mule and he tumbled head over heels into the water.

For a moment he lay there, dazed. Ralph's voice, no more than a croak, roused him.

'Tom? What's wrong? Are you hit?'

Tom tried to sit up and discovered that his legs would not respond. He was not in pain; indeed there seemed to be no sensation at all in the lower half of his body. He hauled himself into a semi-upright position. 'Nothing to worry about. I'll be all right in a minute. Just winded, I think.'

'You fool!' Ralph whispered. 'What did you want to come looking for? I'm finished. Why couldn't you leave me?'

'Don't talk rubbish,' Tom said. 'As if I would. And you're not finished. We're going to get you out.'

'We?'

'There are two more of my chaps out there somewhere. They'll be with us any moment.'

As if in mockery of his words, the moon came out from behind the cloud and the sniper's rifle cracked again. There was no cry of pain and whether anyone had been hit or not Tom had no way of telling.

He dragged his useless legs closer to Ralph. 'Where are you hit?'

'In the guts. There's no point in doing anything. I'm bleeding out.'

Tom dragged a packet of field dressings out of his knapsack. 'You're not giving up as long as I'm with you.'

Ralph's tunic and trousers were ripped across his stomach and when Tom peeled back the ragged edges he revealed a long gash, through which parts of Ralph's intestines were protruding. He unpacked the largest of the dressings and pressed it over the wound. Then, with a struggle, he managed to pass a bandage under Ralph's body and secure it tightly over the dressing; but very quickly both dressing and bandage were dark with blood.

'I told you. It's no good,' Ralph murmured faintly.

'Hold on!' Tom responded. 'Jamieson will be here in a minute with a stretcher.'

Tom was beginning to feel an icy chill seeping up from

somewhere in the lower part of his body. He knew now that he had not just been 'winded'. Something was seriously wrong. It was impossible to move Ralph on his own. All he could do was wait.

After a long silence Ralph whispered, 'Put your arms round me, old friend. I'm chilled to the marrow.'

With difficulty Tom manoeuvred himself nearer and got one arm under Ralph's neck and pulled him close. He felt Ralph burrow his head into his shoulder and laid his cheek against the once-bright hair, now clogged with mud.

'That's better,' Ralph breathed. Then, after another silence, he lifted his head towards Tom's face. 'It was always you, you know. You were the one I really wanted. But I never dared tell you.'

A lunar landscape of missed opportunities spread itself before Tom's imagination. 'But it was the same for me. I wanted you, too, but I was afraid to say so.'

Ralph did not respond for a moment. Then he muttered, 'What a pair of bloody fools!'

'Yes,' Tom agreed, on a sigh. 'Indeed.'

'Too late now,' Ralph said.

'Yes, too late now.'

There was another silence. Then Ralph said, 'It doesn't matter. I wanted you to know. I love you, Tom. I've always loved you. That's all that matters now.'

Tom drew a long breath. 'And I've always loved you. You're right, that's all that really matters.'

This time the silence went on. The moon went behind a cloud again, allowing the stars to shine more brightly. Above the rim of the crater Orion bestrode the heavens and it crossed Tom's mind that he had always intended to find out more about the constellations. Too late for that as well, he reflected. It was clear that Jamieson was not going to appear with the stretcher. Another poor bastard gone down, Tom thought. He wondered if there was such a thing as the afterlife and decided that, if there was, there was a good chance that he and Ralph would enter it together. *In death they were not divided.* Where did that come from? It would make a good epitaph. He wondered if there was any chance that they might be buried in a common grave and hoped that someone would write that on the tombstone. Leo might, if she ever found the place. Leo understood . . .

The moon came out again, lower in the sky now. Somewhere a bird whistled tentatively, as if testing the air for signs of dawn. At some point Tom realized that Ralph was no longer breathing. He closed his eyes and waited for his own moment to arrive.

Fifteen

Leo was busier than she would ever have believed possible. Her fund-raising activities had caught the public imagination and after the initial lecture she found herself being asked to speak at venues up and down the country. With Victoria at her side she travelled to Manchester and Leeds, to Bath and Tunbridge Wells and Oxford. Mabel Stobart lent her influence to promote the campaign and the money rolled in. Soon the hallway at Sussex Gardens was stacked with crates of jam and sugar and packing cases full of hand-knitted socks and balaclava helmets. One morning towards the end of October, in a pause in her travels, Leo looked them over and turned to Victoria.

'Vita, this is crazy. It will be winter soon and that is when all this stuff is going to be needed. There's no point in us turning up with it next spring. We need to get it out there as soon as possible.'

'I take your point,' Victoria said. 'The next question is, how do we get it there? There's no way we can lug this lot on and off trains, and anyway, now there's no Orient Express there isn't any direct rail route.'

'No, it'll have to go by sea,' Leo agreed, 'so the sooner we get it shipped the better.'

Over the next days they haunted the offices of various shipping agents but without success. Merchant shipping was in short supply, owing to the depredations of the German U-boat fleet, and most of it had been diverted to the vital North

Atlantic route. No one was going to Salonika. Finally, a sympathetic Italian ship owner agreed to convey the stores as far as Naples and promised that once there his agent would see them trans-shipped on to a vessel going to Athens. Beyond that he could not guarantee anything.

'There's nothing for it,' Leo said. 'We shall have to go to Athens and wait for it. I'm sure we can find someone there who will take it on the last leg.'

'So how do we get there?' Victoria asked. 'I presume you don't intend to travel on the ship with it.'

'No, that would just be a waste of time. We need to leave just soon enough to be sure we can be there when it arrives.'

'Well, one thing is for sure,' Victoria said, 'we are not driving this time!'

Leo laughed. 'No, I wasn't going to suggest that. We shall have to go by train. I wonder what the best route is.'

'Tell you what: Stobart brought her people back from Albania, didn't she? Let's ask her how they did it.'

Mabel Stobart was able to supply the answer immediately. 'You need to get to Paris. From there you can get a through train to Rome. Then another train down to Brindisi. Of course, you won't be doing the short hop across the Adriatic to Albania, but I'm sure there will be ships going from there to Athens.'

So it was agreed and they began to plan their journey. Leo felt a thrill of excitement that she had not known for many months. Common sense told her that in the current situation she could do no more towards finding her daughter from Salonika than she could from London, but she could not banish the feeling that once there she would be in a position to take advantage of any move forward on that front – perhaps even persuade the generals to make a fresh attempt to liberate Lavci.

Then, one morning, the telegraph boy rang the bell.

Victoria found Leo sitting on a crate in the hall with the telegram still in her hand. 'Leo! What is it?' She crossed to sit beside her and took the telegram from her. '"Regret to inform you your brother Major R.J. Malham Brown is missing in action, believed killed." Oh, Leo! I am so sorry, my dear.'

Leo sighed deeply. 'How many times have we had to say that? Is there no end to the killing?'

'It must come, sooner or later.'

'Not soon enough for Ralph.' She ran her hand over her eyes. 'I can't believe he's dead, Vita. Not Ralph! He was so vital, so indestructible. I can still see him before he went off to the front, shining and eager and . . .' She broke off, struggling for control. 'Do you know, I haven't seen him since that night when we waved them off at the very beginning of the war?'

'Surely . . .? Not once since then?'

'No. By the time he got his first leave I was on my way to Serbia. And since I've been back he hasn't been able to get away.'

'Oh, that's . . . that's very sad.'

Leo looked at her. 'You never liked him much, did you?'

Victoria averted her eyes. 'Not at first, perhaps. But you remember I told you we met in London, after he was wounded? I thought he was much . . . well, we got on quite well . . . that is, up to a point . . .'

Leo blew her nose. 'Well, that's the end of the Malham Browns. Now it looks as if neither of us will leave anything behind for the next generation.'

Victoria got up and moved away. 'Don't, Leo! Please don't talk like that.' There was a harshness in her tone that surprised Leo. She added, more gently, 'You don't know that. We'll find your daughter, one day.'

'Will we?' Leo was absorbed by the sense of lost possibilities. 'What a pity he didn't marry before he left. He was always on at me and Tom to name the day, but I never thought of pressing him to do the same.'

'There was never any question of that, was there?' Victoria said. 'I don't remember him ever having a girlfriend.'

'Oh, there were always girls flirting with him. But as far as I know he was never serious about any of them.'

'That's what I thought,' Victoria murmured. 'But didn't you ever wonder . . .'

Leo looked up suddenly. 'Tom! You don't suppose, do you . . .'

'Suppose what?'

'Do you think he might have been killed, too?'

'Of course not. Why should you think that?'

'Tom was in the same company and I know he would have tried to stick as close to Ralph as possible. So if Ralph was hit . . .'

'There's no reason to assume that Tom was too.'

'But I wouldn't know, would I? Any telegram would go to his mother, and I doubt very much whether she would think to get in touch with me. I'm not sure she even knows we're supposed to be engaged.'

'I'm sure Tom will have thought of that. He will have made some arrangement. Anyway, no news is good news.' Victoria put her hand on Leo's shoulder and shook it gently. 'Come on, old thing! Don't make things worse than they are.'

Leo sighed again and got up. 'You're right. We just have to get on with what we can do for the living. Let's finish packing these crates.'

Two days later a letter arrived for Leo from Frobisher and Weatherby, Solicitors.

> *Dear Miss Malham Brown,*
>
> *We are solicitors acting for Sir Thomas Devenish, Bart. Pursuant to his instructions, I have to inform you, with regret, that Sir Thomas has been wounded in action. The wound, we understand, is serious but not fatal and Sir Thomas is being returned to England for treatment. He is expected to arrive at the Charing Cross Hospital sometime in the next day or two . . .*

'Serious but not fatal!' Leo held the letter out to Victoria. 'Oh, thank God! Thank God!'

A phone call to the hospital elicited the information that they had no Lt Devenish registered at that time, but were expecting a hospital train that evening. First thing the next morning Leo was at the reception desk, among a crowd of other relatives. A harassed clerk told her that Lt Devenish had been brought in the previous evening, but when she hurried up to the ward a sister, whose starched apron was already smudged with blood, informed her curtly that visiting hours were from 2.30 p.m. to four o'clock; and anyway, Lt Devenish was going to be operated on that morning.

'Are you a relative?'

'I'm his fiancée.' She had never realized how useful that spurious title might be.

'You can come back this afternoon if you like. But I don't expect he will be conscious enough to speak to you.'

'Can I ask how badly he is wounded?'

'A bullet is lodged at the base of his spine. We will not know how serious the damage is until after the operation.'

'Can't I see him, just for a moment, before he goes to theatre?'

'No, I'm sorry. If I let you on the ward I should have to let all the other visitors on and then we should never get through the work. I'll tell him you were here. That's the best I can do. What name shall I say?'

'Leo. Just Leo.'

At 2.30 p.m. Leo was back at the hospital, in company with a crowd of mothers and wives carrying bunches of flowers and bags of grapes.

A different sister glanced down a list of patients and said doubtfully, 'Lieutenant Devenish is back from theatre, but I think you'll find he's still very woozy. You can sit with him if you like but he may not know you're there.'

Leo walked down the ward, between the long rows of beds with their tightly drawn white bedcovers, in an atmosphere that was at once familiar and alien. The men lying in the beds reminded her of Lozengrad and Adrianople. She had seen similar wounds there; similar expressions on their faces of pain or long-suffering courage. But the smells and squalor of Adrianople were missing, replaced by immaculate cleanliness, and the atmosphere of cheerful banter she recalled from Lozengrad had been replaced by a sense of military discipline which hushed the voices of patients and visitors alike. It was impossible to imagine these men sitting up to shout 'Mellie Chissimas!'

The screens were drawn round Tom's bed and on passing through them she was shocked by his appearance. His face was as white as the pillow, the skin drawn tight over his skull so that his nose and cheekbones looked razor sharp, and the whites of his eyes showed between half-closed lids. She had seen men close to death look like this. She leaned over him and stroked his cheek.

'Tom? It's Leo. You're in hospital. You've been hurt, but you're going to be all right.'

The eyelids fluttered and the cracked lips moved soundlessly. She understood what he wanted. An enamel mug of water stood on the locker by the bed and she slid an arm under his neck and raised his head so that he could take a sip.

'No more now. You can have more later.'

She watched him struggling back to consciousness, saw the signs of mounting nausea and supported him while he vomited, then wiped his lips with her handkerchief. His eyes were fully open now.

'Ralph!' It was a hoarse whisper.

'It's all right. Don't try to talk yet.'

'Ralph's dead.'

'Yes. I know, my dear. I'm so sorry.'

He was silent for a while, and when he spoke his voice was stronger. 'He died in my arms, Leo. He wasn't alone.'

She swallowed a sob. 'I'm glad. That would have meant a lot to him.'

'I tried to get him back. I was looking for him . . . but he was too badly hurt . . . and then . . .'

'You were wounded trying to save him. Of course, I should have known. Bless you, Tom.'

He seemed to slip back into sleep and she sat for some time, holding his hand in silence. Then he opened his eyes again. 'I should have gone with him. I thought we were going together.'

'But you didn't. You're alive, thank God.'

The expression on his face was so bleak that it caught at her heart. 'I should have gone too,' he repeated.

'No!' she replied. 'No, Tom. You had to stay alive for me. I need you, Tom. I don't know what I'd do without you.'

The words were out of her mouth before she realized that they were truer than she had ever imagined.

He slept again then, until the bell rang for the end of visiting hours.

The following afternoon the sister drew her aside from the

crowd of other visitors. 'I understand you are Lieutenant Devenish's fiancée. Is that correct?'

'Yes.'

'I thought I ought to warn you. The surgeons say it is very unlikely that he will ever walk again.'

Leo nodded. The news did not come as a shock. She had dealt with men wounded in that way before. 'Does he know?'

'Yes. The surgeon spoke to him this morning.'

'I'll go and sit with him.'

Walking down the ward she tried to imagine how Tom was feeling. What could she say that might be of some comfort? He was propped up on pillows and the death's head look had gone, but his eyes were blank and he did not smile as she bent to kiss his cheek.

'Have they told you?'

'Yes. I'm sorry, my dear. It's a rotten thing to happen, but it could have been much worse. We both know that.'

He stared ahead without expression. 'It doesn't matter. I should have gone with Ralph. That's what I wanted. Why didn't they leave me with him?'

'How could they? You were alive, and every life is valuable. You mustn't blame yourself, Tom. You did everything you could, and you were with him at the end. He must have found that a great comfort. Now you have to think of your own life. You must get well and strong again, and then we'll make plans for the best way to deal with this.'

'We?' he said.

'Of course. I'm not going to let you cope with this on your own.'

He looked at her then and she saw a flicker of life in his eyes. 'Dear Leo! But you mustn't throw yourself away on a lost cause. You've got more important things to do.'

'You are not a lost cause! And I don't want to hear any more of that sort of talk. I thought you were made of sterner stuff, Tom Devenish!'

He dropped his gaze and she thought her words had gone home, but he said nothing more.

After a moment she went on: 'Does your mother know you are here?'

'I suppose she will have been told. But I doubt if she has understood. How did you know?'

'Your solicitors wrote to me.'

'Of course, I remember. I told them to get in touch if anything . . .'

'I'm glad you did.'

There seemed to be no more to say and after a moment he closed his eyes and fell asleep. Leo sat on for a while, busy with her own thoughts. Then she got up, kissed him lightly on the forehead and set off back to Sussex Gardens.

'Vita, I can't go!'

'What? Can't go where?'

Victoria looked up from a pile of paperwork.

'I can't go to Salonika. Not now. Not yet. Tom is going to need me and I can't let him down.'

'Why? How bad is it?'

'They say he won't walk again. But I don't think that is what is troubling him. He thinks he should have died with Ralph. He hasn't really taken the rest of it in yet. But you do see, don't you? I can't leave him.'

'Yes, I see that,' Victoria responded, frowning. 'But that lot in the hall is being collected the day after tomorrow and we can't leave it to rot on the docks in the Piraeus. Someone has to arrange for it to be trans-shipped.'

'There must be someone we could contact. Maybe my father's old friend at the FO could suggest something.'

'No need.' Victoria got up decisively. 'I'll go. You can follow on later when you've got Tom settled somewhere.'

'You can't go all that way on your own!'

Victoria gave a derisive laugh. 'Oh, come on, Leo! It wouldn't be the first time. I got back on my own from our last little expedition, if you remember.'

'Of course I remember. But I still don't like to think of you having to cope with everything by yourself.'

'I'll be fine. After all, Athens isn't exactly the back of beyond. I'll arrange for the stuff to be transported to Salonika and go with it to make sure it's distributed to the right people. Then I'll wait for you to join me. You do still plan to go eventually?'

'Of course I do!' Leo sat down and rested her head on her hands. For days she had been buoyed up by the thought that soon she would be back in Salonika, ready to seize the first opportunity to head for Bitola and the village where she had been parted from her baby. Now she would have to wait longer. 'You know how much I want to get out there. But I have a duty to Tom, too.'

'Yes, I know,' Victoria agreed. She put her hand on Leo's shoulder. 'After all, a few weeks won't make much difference. I can see that the troops get their comforts and we wouldn't be able to do anything else until the spring comes. You can stay here with Tom until after Christmas and still be in Salonika in plenty of time.'

Leo nodded unwillingly. 'I suppose it makes sense, but I'm not happy about leaving it all to you.'

'Don't worry about me,' her friend said. 'I'll be fine.'

The following morning Leo was busy putting the labels on the last crates when the doorbell rang. Beavis opened the front door to reveal Luke on the doorstep. She jumped up and ran to him.

'Luke! You're in civvies. What has happened?'

It was only then that she saw how pale he was and how sore and red his eyes appeared. He took the hand she offered and said, in an uncharacteristically husky voice, 'Got a whiff of some new gas the Jerries are using. The medics reckon I'm not fit for active service any more. So here I am, a free man, just waiting for a boat to take me back home.'

'Oh, Luke. How awful!'

He shook his head with a grin. 'Don't look like that. It's not life-threatening. They reckon with time I'll be fine. But it's bought me my ticket home.'

'I don't know whether to sympathize or congratulate you,' Leo said. 'But speaking personally I'm just very glad that you are out of it. At least one person I care about is going to survive.' She drew him into the house. 'Come on in and sit down. Beavis, can we have some coffee, please? Come into the morning room. There's a fire in there.'

When they were seated in front of the fire he said, 'You said something about one person you cared for being safe. Does that mean you've lost someone?'

'My brother, Ralph,' Leo said. It was hard to put it into words, even now. 'Killed in action, not far from where you have been until lately, I imagine.'

'Poor fellow!' Luke said. 'I'm really sorry to hear that, Leo.'

Leo sighed. 'I suppose it was inevitable. He had been in the fighting right from the beginning. It's a miracle that he survived so long. So many didn't. Soldiering was his whole life, so at least he died doing what he regarded as his duty. In some ways it's harder for the survivors.' She went on to tell him about Tom's condition.

Luke shook his head with a sigh. 'I never met Tom, or your brother, but I feel I almost did from reading your letters. I don't know which one to be more sorry for. I guess in some ways Tom has the worst deal.'

'That's what I meant. But I'm determined not to let him feel that way. Tom's alive and I'm going to make sure he's grateful for every extra day.'

'Well, he's lucky to have you to help him.' He paused. 'Didn't you tell me once that you and he were engaged?'

'We still are,' Leo said, 'but that's another story. Have another cup of coffee?'

Her tone effectively put an end to that topic of conversation, as she had intended.

After a moment's silence Luke said, 'What's all that stuff in the hallway. Are you moving out, Leo?'

She smiled, glad of the chance to change the subject. 'No. Not yet, anyway. It's comforts for the troops out in Salonika.' She went on to explain about her fund-raising efforts and the arrangements she had made for the shipping of the goods. 'The trouble is,' she ended, 'there is no one to oversee the last leg of the journey. Victoria and I were going out to Athens, but now I can't leave Tom.'

At that moment Beavis announced Victoria. Luke heaved himself to his feet and held out his hand.

Victoria stopped short and Leo saw her colour come and go. Then she came forward and shook Luke's hand in a manner that struck Leo as being unnecessarily formal. Luke explained again how he came to be there and when they were settled and Beavis had been despatched for fresh coffee he said, 'Leo has been telling me about the goods you are sending out to Salonika. I think it's a splendid idea. Lord knows those fellows get little enough in the way of home comforts. But I gather you have a problem getting them there from Athens, now Leo feels she has to stay in London.'

'That's solved.' Victoria said. 'I'm going on my own.'

Leo saw Luke straighten in his seat. 'Not while I can stand on two feet, you won't! I'll come with you.'

She caught her breath. 'Luke, you can't. You're supposed to be going home.'

'So what? I can go home via Salonika. It's almost on the way.'

Victoria patted her bad leg and jerked her chin towards Luke. 'Didn't you tell me you got wounded in the leg on Gallipoli? I've heard of the blind leading the blind, but isn't this going to be a case of the lame helping the lame?'

He grinned. 'Exactly. We can compensate for each other's deficiencies. At least we've got two good legs between us.'

'What are we preparing for – a three-legged race?' she flashed back.

'Oh, come on, Vicky,' he said. 'It'll be like old times. What do you say?'

She looked at him with narrowed eyes. 'On one condition.'

'Which is?'

'That you promise never, ever to call me Vicky again.'

He laughed. 'You win. I promise.'

Leo said, 'Are you sure you're up to it, Luke – joking apart? I'd be much happier in my own mind knowing you were with Vita, but it won't help if your health gives way.'

'I'll be fine,' he assured her. 'Now I've had a chance to rest up I'm improving every day.'

Leo still had doubts about the whole enterprise but it quickly became clear that, in spite of her initial reaction, Victoria was as keen on the idea as Luke was and between them they overrode her arguments. The next day they saw the crates loaded on to a lorry and followed them to the docks, where they were winched on board a freighter.

There followed a period of relative inactivity, which Leo

filled with daily visits to Tom in hospital. His physical condition improved slowly, but she was increasingly worried by his mental state. She took him books and newspapers, which he did not open, so she resorted to reading aloud to him. He showed some interest in news from the battle front, but the attacks had finally been called off on November the twelfth, with little ground gained in exchange for the thousands of lives that had been sacrificed. Another winter of stalemate faced the exhausted troops and there was little in the news to cheer anyone. Seeking some light relief, she began reading him Jerome K. Jerome's *Three Men in a Boat*. This raised the occasional pale smile but after a few pages it was clear that he was no longer listening. The only time she felt she really had his attention was when she took in a recently published book of poetry by Robert Graves. When she read him 'The Morning before the Battle' he nodded slowly and said, 'That is the work of someone who understands because he's been there. Only someone like that can salvage something worthwhile out of the chaos.'

Early in December Victoria and Luke left on the first leg of their journey. Preoccupied with Tom, Leo had scarcely noticed how much time they were spending together but as she saw them off at the station she became aware that there had been developments in their relationship. Victoria no longer seemed on the defensive and much of the old camaraderie had returned, but there was a deeper undercurrent. They still laughed and teased each other but there was a quiet understanding in their eyes that suggested neither of them was going to repeat their earlier mistakes.

Left on her own, Leo sank back into her previous lethargy. Over the previous months the hard work of organizing the fund-raising and travelling to speaking engagements, and subsequently her visits to Tom, had allowed her to put her own tragedy to the back of her mind. Now the memory of Sasha's death and the loss of her daughter were joined by the full realization of her brother's death. He was her only relative and without him she was completely alone in the world. She remembered the adventures they had shared growing up together and the bitter disagreements that had followed. At

least they had parted on good terms, but even that reconcili-
ation had been based on a deceit – the deceit that she and
Tom intended to marry. Now Tom was all that was left of her
old life and she was beginning to doubt whether he would
ever recover fully. Striving to throw off her own depression,
it was doubly hard to find ways to raise his spirits.

Soon after Victoria and Luke's departure Tom was discharged
from hospital and sent to a private nursing home in Surrey to
recuperate. Victoria had left Sparky in Leo's care, so she was
able to drive down to visit him every few days. The journey
through the darkening country lanes, where the rain dripped
endlessly from the leafless trees, seemed to Leo to symbolize
everything she felt.

Then, one afternoon, she arrived to find Tom in the unheated
conservatory, wrapped to the chin in blankets and sweaters,
sitting in his wheelchair in front of an easel, with a brush in
one hand and palette in the other.

She hurried to kiss his cheek. 'Tom, you're painting again!
I'm so pleased!'

He looked up at her with a small, wry smile. 'I woke up
yesterday morning and realized I was wallowing in self-pity and
there was no justification for it. I can still see and I have the
use of both my arms. So I can paint, which is all I have ever
wanted to do. Besides,' he indicated the canvas in front of him,
'there are things I need to get off my chest.'

Leo saw the half-formed outlines of bodies, lying in contorted
heaps, and shuddered. But she squeezed his shoulder. 'Yes,
you're right. People need to see what you've seen, and you
need to show them. Well done, my dear!'

He reached for her hand. 'I've drawn on you for comfort,
at a time when I should have been trying to give it instead.
I'm sorry.'

'There's nothing to be sorry for. All I want is to see you
get back to your old self. And now I can see you're on the
mend.'

'Thanks to you.' He kissed her hand. 'You're freezing! Let's
go back inside and get warm. I can get on with this later.'

The following day Leo received a telegram. *Arrived in Athens
safely. Awaiting arrival of goods, love V and L.*

Back at the nursing home she found Tom had been hard at work on his painting but it worried her that the cold conservatory was not a good place for a convalescent. He pre-empted her concern, however, by saying, 'The people here are dropping hints that it's time I moved out and made room for someone in greater need.'

'But where can you go?' Leo asked. 'You can't possibly live alone. You need help with so many basic things.'

'I know,' he said ruefully, 'and before you even think of volunteering, the answer is no. I won't let you burden yourself with all that. Besides, it's not a woman's job.'

'No,' Leo agreed. 'What you need is a male nurse, or a manservant who has some experience in that direction.'

'A gentleman's gentleman,' he said. 'That's what I was thinking.'

'Didn't you have someone, before the war?'

'Peters – yes. He volunteered to enlist with me, with a view to becoming my orderly, but he had flat feet, apparently, and they wouldn't take him. But I heard from him later. When conscription came in it seems his feet weren't as flat as the first MO thought – anyway, they were good enough for cannon fodder. I had a letter from his mother, last summer. He was killed on the Somme.'

'Oh,' Leo said. One more death out of so many warranted no further comment. 'Well, we need to find you someone else. I'll put an advert in the papers. But if you leave here, where will you go?'

'Denham, I suppose. There's just about room for me and a servant in the Dower House with mother, and I suppose I ought to spend some time with her.'

'Have you heard from her?'

'She occasionally sends me parcels. I think she believes I am still at the front.'

'Oh dear! That isn't going to be an ideal arrangement, is it?'

'No, but the house in Cheyne Walk is let for the duration, and anyway it's hardly suitable with all those stairs. I think I'll see if the current tenants want to buy, and then I can get a flat. But until then it will have to be Denham.'

'Well, at least we can find you someone congenial to look after you,' Leo said. 'Leave that to me.'

Glad to have a new project, Leo placed advertisements in the situations vacant columns of several newspapers, though without much optimism. With so many dead and others away at the front there were far too few men available to fill the vacancies. However, she was pleasantly surprised by the response and, after a series of interviews, she whittled the applicants down to three and arranged to take them down to Surrey for Tom to make the final choice. It gave her some satisfaction to learn that he had picked the man she herself would have chosen.

Arnold Simpson, Sim as he begged to be called, was twenty-seven years old, a sturdy, broad-shouldered young man with a ruddy countryman's complexion marred by a deep scar that ran from the corner of one eye to his jawbone. He had left school at fourteen and gone into service in a country house in the Cotswolds but after several years there had been offered a job as valet and general help to a doctor with a prosperous practice in Cheltenham. When the doctor had volunteered to serve with the army Sim had gone with him as his orderly and had served as his right-hand man when dealing with casualties. The doctor had been killed during the battle of Loos and Sim had gone on to work as a medical orderly, until he in his turn was hit by a sniper's bullet which had gone into his back below the shoulder blade, come out by his collarbone and carved the scar on his face. That was six months ago, and though he had been discharged on medical grounds because the bullet had clipped his lung, he declared himself fully fit and able to do all that Tom might require. Apart from the obvious relevance of his experience in the field, there were several things that recommended him to both Leo and Tom. First was an indomitable cheerfulness, a quality that they both felt much in need of. Also, in spite of his lack of formal education, it was clear that he was highly intelligent – something the doctor who employed him had obviously spotted because, as Sim himself said, he had taught him more during their years together than any amount of schooling. The doctor had been a man of wide interests and much of that had rubbed off on Sim and his country upbringing had given him much in common with Tom. He showed an immediate interest in Tom's paintings and, having lived through the same horrors, was able to relate to them in a way that was impossible for Leo. As a final bonus, he was not employed and could start work immediately.

A week before Christmas Leo hired a brand-new Rolls-Royce motor car, Sparky in her opinion being neither commodious nor reliable enough for the job. She collected Sim from the station and drove him down to the nursing home. There they helped Tom into the car, put his wheelchair in the boot and set off for Denham.

Sixteen

Leo spent Christmas at the Dower House with Tom. It was a less-than-ideal arrangement. The house was really too small for all of them and a bed had to be moved down to the study, the only room on the ground floor which could accommodate Tom without disrupting the rest of the household. With the three servants plus Leo and Lady Devenish, every room in the house was occupied, but what was more important, in Leo's mind, was the fact that there was nowhere convenient for Tom to paint.

Lady Devenish's hold on reality was becoming noticeably more fragile. She seemed unable to remember why Tom was in a wheelchair. Sometimes she reverted to the time when he was a baby in a pushchair and thought Leo was his nursemaid. Once she chided him petulantly for not standing up when she entered the room. Tom treated her with patience and courtesy but Leo could detect no warmth in their relationship. It seemed that the close bond that should exist between mother and son had broken down – if it had ever existed.

On Christmas Eve Tom asked Sim to push him up the drive to the big house and Leo went with them. The house had been bought by a developer who intended to turn it into flats but so far it remained empty, the paint peeling and the windows veiled with cobwebs. After they had walked all round and peered into the empty rooms Tom sighed.

'You know, when I was a boy this place would have been alight with candles and decorations at this time of year. My father always gave a big party on Boxing Day and invited half the county. He was still doing it, right up to last year – on borrowed money, of course. But they were all glad to come and eat and drink at his expense, and now there hasn't been so much as a Christmas card from any of them. Nothing like a bankruptcy and a suicide to wipe you off the social map!'

One regular visitor to the Dower House, they learned from Lowndes, had been the local vicar, so out of gratitude to him rather than religious conviction, they all went to Matins on Christmas morning. As they made their way down the aisle towards the family pew at the front of the church Leo was conscious of heads turning in their direction and whispers passing along the rows. Out of habit, Lady Devenish smiled vaguely and bowed to left and right, but her eyes lacked focus. Tom stared straight ahead. At the end of the service the local gentry seemed inclined to make amends for their neglect and clustered round Tom's wheelchair, mouthing platitudes about 'heroism' and 'duty' and defence of the country. Tom received their plaudits with chilly courtesy and Leo, standing beside him, felt appraising eyes upon her as she was introduced as his fiancée. After that, the invitations did begin to arrive, and all were politely declined.

One good thing came out of the occasion: two days later the vicar called again and took a lively interest in Tom's painting. Lady Devenish presented him with yet another beautifully worked kneeler and he said with a laugh, 'At this rate, every member of the congregation will soon have an embroidered hassock to kneel on. But I have another idea. Perhaps, Sir Thomas, you could design a wall-hanging for your mother to embroider – something that would serve as a memorial to the fallen. What do you think?'

Tom was immediately taken with the idea and it gave Leo some pleasure to see him and his mother with their heads together, examining his preliminary sketches and discussing colours. For the first time, it seemed, they felt a genuine connection.

Once Christmas and New Year were over it became obvious that they could not all continue to live in the Dower House so one evening, when they were sitting alone in front of the fire, Leo drew her chair close to Tom's.

'We can't stay here, Tom. It's too cramped and there is nowhere for you to work. Why don't you move in with me at Sussex Gardens?'

He raised his eyebrows. 'And scandalize the neighbourhood? What about your reputation?'

Leo laughed dryly. 'My dear man, you and I both know that after the life I've led I have no reputation. Anyway, who cares?'

He shook his head. 'It wouldn't be right. I mean, on what basis would I be there? Would I be a lodger or what?'

'Does it matter?'

'Yes, I think it does.'

She was silent for a moment. What she was about to say had been germinating in her mind for some time but she had never formulated it in words until that evening.

'And if we were married? Would that make it all right?'

'Married? You're not serious.'

'Why not? After all, we've been engaged long enough.'

'But we both know that was purely a device. We never intended to marry.'

'Not then, I know. But circumstances are different now.'

'Yes, indeed they are. You know it could never have been a real marriage, for reasons we both understand. But at least then I should not have been a burden to you. Now it is doubly impossible.'

'I know that! You know I'm not expecting anything like that. And you would not be a burden.'

'Yes, I should. And I'm not going to let you throw yourself away looking after me.' He silenced her protest with a gesture. 'You're a beautiful woman, Leo. When this war is over men will be queuing up to pay court to you.'

She gave another brief, ironic laugh. 'After all the deaths there have been, it's the poor spinsters who will be queuing up for any available man that's left. But I shan't be one of them.' She took his hand. 'I've had my one great love affair,

Tom. I don't expect to have another. We've both lost the one person who mattered more to us than anything else in this life. All I want is a companion. We're good friends. We're very fond of each other. Can't we get what consolation we can from that?'

He gave a lopsided smile. 'There was a time when you couldn't stand the sight of me.'

'Only because I thought I was going to be forced to marry you! I'm older and wiser now.'

'But what about children? You could still have children with the right man.'

'I have a child, remember. That's all I want.'

'And you still want to go and look for her?'

'Of course, as soon as the winter is over. I'll have to leave you for a while then, but you have Sim to take care of you.'

He was silent in his turn. Then he said, 'I'll make a bargain with you. I'll move into Sussex Gardens as a tenant to take care of the place while you're away. You go and find your daughter, and when you come back we'll talk about this again – if you still want to. Will that do?'

She kissed his cheek. 'It will have to, for now.'

In the last days of February Leo stood on the pitching deck of a small fishing boat and watched, for the third time, the outline of the city of Salonika take shape in front of her. Memories crowded her mind: sailing in with Victoria, six years ago, thrilling at the start of a great adventure (what a naïve pair they had been then!); returning by land, bitter and resentful, when her brother dragged her back to Belgrade; sailing in again with Mabel Stobart and her team, older and wiser, but still excited by the thought that Sasha was somewhere beyond the mountains, and soon she might meet him again; and then, the summer before last, standing on deck with his arm round her waist, in the first glow of their love affair, convinced that soon they would be marching into Serbia and able to begin the life they had imagined for themselves. How different this return was! And the difference was emphasized by the city itself. Gone were the minarets and domes she remembered and in their places were blackened ruins or empty spaces where land had been cleared but not yet built on. It was a tragic irony, she thought, that this disaster had not been the result of war, but rather of an army kept too long away from the fighting; for she was sure in her own mind that the fire must have been the result of some drunken revelry of a kind she had seen often during her last stay.

Her reverie was broken by the sight of familiar faces on the dockside. Victoria and Luke were waving excitedly and very soon she was embracing them both.

'How are you? Are you exhausted? The sea's really rough today. Were you sick?'

'No, I'm fine. You know me. I'm never seasick.'

'How's Tom?'

'He's doing really well. He's started painting again and we've found an excellent man to look after him. He's going to be all right.'

Her luggage was loaded into a horse-drawn cab and they set off through the city. As they drove Victoria told her how they had distributed half the extra food and clothing to the Serbian soldiers in the garrison on the morning of the Orthodox Christmas.

'You should have seen their faces! It was heartbreaking in a way to see how pathetically grateful they were. But they were so thrilled. I saw one officer line up his whole platoon and go along the line giving each man a spoonful of jam. They looked as if they were being given manna from heaven! I made sure they knew it was from you, and how hard you had worked to get the money. General Bojovic wants to thank you personally.'

Listening to her, Leo thought that it was a long time since she had seen her so animated. This new expedition had been good for her. Perhaps, she reflected, she had needed to get away from London. Luke said little, but his ready, boyish grin had returned.

'And you have kept plenty back for the men in Bitola?' she said.

'Oh, yes. But the road is still closed through the mountains. We shall have to wait until spring to deliver that.'

They arrived at length at a small hotel on the outskirts of the city.

'It's not very grand, I'm afraid,' Luke said, 'but accommodation is hard to find since the fire.'

'This will do perfectly,' Leo said, glad that there was nothing here to remind her of the room she had shared with Sasha through those blissful summer days.

That night at dinner she began to realize that the excitement she had sensed in Victoria and to a lesser extent in Luke was not simply the result of the success of their mission. Nevertheless, she was stunned when Luke said, 'Leo, there's something we have to tell you. Victoria and I are going to be married.'

'Married!' Leo put down the wine glass she had been about to raise to her lips. So many questions crowded into her mind that for a moment she was unable to speak, but the glow on her friends' faces was irresistible. She got up and went round the table to kiss them both. 'I'm so pleased for both of you. You're made for each other. I'm sure you will be very happy.'

'It wasn't an easy decision for either of us,' Luke said. 'After all, I'm asking Vita to move to a distant country and take on a ready-made family. But Anton and Nadia really need a mother.'

'Yes, I can see the difficulty,' Leo said. 'But I presume you're happy with it, Vita?'

'The distant country, or the ready-made family?' Victoria asked with a smile.

'Well, both.'

'I know I told you years ago that I wouldn't consider moving to the other side of the world, but things are different now. I'm different. My wild motor-racing days are over and what I really want now is a bit of peace and stability. And Luke has convinced me that life in New Zealand can be wonderful. To hear him talk about it, you would think it was an earthly paradise.'

'So it is,' Luke chipped in.

'As to the family . . . well, I've never thought of myself as the maternal type, but I'm willing to give it a try. I just hope they take to me.'

'Of course they will,' Luke said. 'And there's still time for another addition.'

Leo saw a shadow cross Victoria's face. 'That's . . . well, we'll have to wait and see.'

'I wish you every happiness,' Leo said, but a chill was beginning to creep round her heart at the thought of losing her
friend. 'I just wish you weren't going to be so far away.'

'As to that,' Luke said, 'you made me a promise years ago that
you would come out and visit. I'm going to hold you to it.'

'Yes, you must come,' Victoria added. 'And bring Alexandra
with you. You never know, you might decide to settle there
too.'

'It's good horse country,' Luke put in.

Leo smiled. 'I will come, one day. I promise. When do you
plan to leave?'

'Not until you've found your daughter,' he said. 'We won't
leave you to search on your own.'

Alone in her room that night, Leo tried to reconcile herself
to the news. She knew she should be glad for Victoria and
reminded herself that years ago in Adrianople she had been
furious with her for refusing Luke's proposal. But she could
not rid herself of the feeling that yet another one of those
dearest to her was being taken away.

When Victoria came into her room to wake her next
morning she found her standing at the window with tears
running down her face.

'Oh, my dear, what is it? What's wrong?' Victoria put her
arm round Leo's shoulders. 'It's not because of me and Luke,
is it?'

'No, no,' Leo assured her, wiping her eyes. 'I just realized
that it is a year ago to the day that Alexandra was born . . .
and that Sasha died.'

'Oh, love! I didn't know. I'm sorry.'

'How could you know? I had to work out the dates myself.
It was all so confused. But I'm sure it's right. My baby is one
year old today.'

Victoria squeezed her shoulders. 'Soon the snow will begin
to melt and we'll be able to get through to Bitola and, who
knows, to Lavci too. When we find her we'll have the best
birthday party we can possibly arrange.'

Later that day Leo went to call on General Bojovic and
receive his thanks for her efforts. 'What is the chance of a new
campaign this summer?' she asked.

'Undoubtedly there will be another attempt to break out,' he assured her. 'And this time we shall succeed. My intelligence suggests that the Bulgarians have had enough of the fighting. It is only the backing of the Austrians and the Germans that keeps them in the field. By the end of the summer we shall be back in Belgrade.'

Leo smiled and thanked him, but inwardly she was remembering how the same sentiments had been expressed two years earlier.

'I have a little surprise for you,' the general said. 'Come with me.'

He led her down to the courtyard of the house he was occupying and shouted an order. A soldier appeared leading a small chestnut horse.

'It's Star!' Leo exclaimed. 'How did she get here?'

'She was sent back from Bitola at the same time as you, and I have made sure she was looked after. I knew you would return some day.'

Leo was tempted to throw her arms round the general but checked the impulse in case it was seen as bad for discipline. So she ran down the steps from the door and embraced the horse instead. Star nuzzled her pocket and whickered softly and Leo allowed herself to believe that the little mare remembered her.

'Thank you, General!' she said. 'Thank you so much. I can't tell you how much this means to me.'

Over the following days Leo renewed her acquaintanceship with a number of old friends. They all expressed their delight at seeing her back, looking fit and well, and tactfully sympathized over Sasha's death. Victoria and Luke had already made arrangements to borrow mounts from the French cavalry regiment stationed in the city and the three of them rode out every morning. In the evening they were often invited to dine with various officers and their families or with local residents. It was not unlike the happy days Leo had spent there before, but she could take very little pleasure in it. Each morning she looked out of her window at the distant mountains and hoped to see signs of the snow melting, but winter seemed reluctant to relax its grip.

At long last a messenger arrived from Bitola: the road was open again and the town was desperately in need of supplies. Leo, Victoria and Luke left in the first convoy, in a car loaned by the general himself, escorted by a detachment of Serbian troops. It was a long, hard drive, over roads flooded by the melting snow, and when they came in sight of the town Leo had to suppress a cry of distress. Bitola had been battered when she was there the previous winter, but now there was hardly a building standing. It seemed hard to imagine how the garrison had held out so long.

They found Dr Pierre Leseaux still at work in what remained of the hospital. He was thin and worn and looked ten years older, but he greeted Leo with his usual warmth.

'*Bienvenue, ma chère!* I am so glad to see you well again. Really, the transformation is amazing. When I sent you off back to Salonika I was not sure that you would survive the journey.'

'I wouldn't have survived at all if you hadn't found me and pulled me out of that snow drift,' Leo said. 'Patty told me how you saved my life.'

'Ah, Patty! Do you hear from her? How is she?'

'She's nursing in France. She writes when she can and when I last heard she was well.' She turned to introduce her two companions and Pierre shook their hands warmly.

'I am afraid I can offer you very little in the way of hospitality, but now that the supplies have arrived perhaps we can manage a good dinner.'

'Please don't worry about us,' Victoria said. 'We've both worked at the front in various places, so we're used to roughing it. And we're not here as guests. We'll work for our keep. I've been driving ambulances and Luke has worked as a stretcher-bearer, so we can both make ourselves useful.'

'And of course I'll help out, too,' Leo said. 'I'm sure you can do with extra hands.'

'Always!' the doctor agreed. 'The bombardment of the city seems to have stopped, for the time being at least. But we still have casualties to care for, and there are many cases of frostbite and general sickness of one kind and another. But you did not come here for that, I know. Leo, can you forgive me for what

I did? I had to find someone to care for your baby, or she
would have died. I hope you understand that.'

'I do, now,' Leo said slowly. 'But did you have to send me
away?'

'I sent you to Salonika because I felt we could not care for
you properly here. It was not my decision to put you on that
hospital ship for England. But perhaps it was for the best. You
would not have regained your health so quickly here. Now,
you have come back to search for your child, but alas, I have
to tell you that Lavci is still in Bulgarian hands.'

This was a blow, but not unexpected. 'Has there been any
communication?' Leo asked. 'Is there any chance of getting a
message to the family?'

'I fear not. The area has changed hands several times over
the last year but at the moment all the approaches are guarded
by Bulgarian troops.'

'General Bojovic assures me that there will be a new attempt
to break through this summer,' Leo said. 'I suppose I must just
try to be patient.'

They had brought the best that Salonika could offer in the
way of wine and provisions with them and that evening they
sat down with Pierre and what remained of his staff to a better
meal than the beleaguered medical team had seen for months.
There was taramasalata and artichokes, and roast suckling pig
and the first fresh green vegetables of the year, and pastries
rich with almonds and honey. As the wine bottles emptied
there was a general air of celebration, but Leo could only think
of the village a few miles away up the mountain road and
wonder how long it would be before she could reach it.

The next day they presented the comforts they had brought
from England to the Serbian troops in the garrison and saw
their pinched, half-starved faces light up.

'It's so little,' Leo said with a sigh. 'But it means a lot to
them.'

After that, it was back to the familiar routine of work in
the hospital and the apparently endless wait for something to
happen.

Then one day they heard that there had been renewed
fighting along the River Vardar and in the Struma area. It

seemed the summer offensive had started at last. A week later a messenger rode into town and the commandant of the garrison sent word that he would like to see Leo as soon as she was free.

'I have good news for you!' he said as soon as she appeared. 'According to the men I have posted on the heights above Lavci, the Bulgarians are pulling out.'

'Pulling out!' Leo felt she could hardly breathe. 'Why?'

'Perhaps to reinforce their lines elsewhere. I hear they are being pushed back by our troops.'

'Are you sure? Are they all going?'

'It's too soon to tell. But I will keep you informed.'

For three days Leo existed in what felt to her like suspended animation. Then word came that the last Bulgarians had left the village and the road was clear. A small force was sent out to investigate and Leo, with Victoria and Luke beside her, mounted on borrowed horses, went with them. The snow had melted from the lower slopes now and the mountainsides were green with new grass. Acacia blossoms overhung the road and the alpine pastures were starred with tiny pink orchids, but the evidence of the recent conflict was everywhere in the craters left by shells and the debris of broken gun carriages and spent cartridges.

Victoria looked around her. 'This place must have been lovely in peacetime.'

Leo lifted her face to the hills and took in the view for the first time. 'Yes, it must. But how long will it take to restore it to the way it used to be?' She rode in silence for a moment. Then she said, 'Am I doing the right thing, Vita? She's been with this other family for over a year. She will think of that other woman as her mother. Do I have the right to drag her away?'

'She's only a baby,' Victoria said. 'She will soon forget. Just think of how much better her life will be with you. Think of all the advantages you can give her.'

As they rounded the last bend in the road Leo had to put her hand to her mouth to suppress a cry of horror. The village lay ahead of them, but all that remained of it were ruins. Not one single building stood higher than a few courses of the once-sturdy stone walls. As they rode into what had once been the main square there seemed to be no sign of human habitation and Leo gazed around her with a sense of disbelief. All the way up the road she had been preparing herself for meeting her daughter, trying to envisage the scene, wondering how the child would react, what she would look like. And now there was nothing except emptiness.

The captain in charge of their escort shouted, 'Is there anyone here? Come out and show yourselves!'

Somewhere a dog barked, but otherwise the silence was unbroken. Then Leo saw a movement out of the corner of her eye. An old man appeared at the top of some steps leading down to a cellar.

'You! Come here,' the captain called. 'Are you the only one left here?'

The old man spat on the ground. 'What do you want? Soldiers! You're all the same.'

The captain urged his horse forward and it looked as if he might strike the old man but Leo put her own mount between them. 'Please, I'm looking for someone. Do you know the Popovic family?'

'Popovic?' He squinted up at her. 'The ones who took in the English lady's baby – the one who died?'

Leo felt a hand tighten round her throat. 'The baby died?'

'No, not the baby. The woman. Came here for some reason, gave birth and died.'

'No!' Leo said. 'No, she didn't die! I'm that woman. I've come to find my baby. Please, do you know where the Popovics are?'

He jerked his head towards a heap of rubble that had once been a house.

'That was their place.'

'And what happened to them?'

He shrugged. 'Direct hit. No chance.'

Leo drooped over the neck of her horse. For a moment she thought she was going to faint. Then she heard a woman's voice.

'What is it? What do they want, Janachko?' An old woman had joined the man.

'Looking for the Popovics.' He jerked his head towards Leo. 'She's the mother of the child they took in. I've told her the whole family bought it when that shell hit their house.'

'No, they didn't! You silly old fool.' She hobbled to the side of Leo's horse. 'He doesn't know what he's talking about. They left weeks before that shell hit. They went north to get away from the fighting.'

'Are you sure?' Leo could feel the blood pulsing in her head. 'Where did they go?'

'They were here!' the old man insisted. 'It was that other lot from next door who left.'

'No, it wasn't! Don't pay any attention to him, my lady. They went north and took your baby with them.'

Others had appeared from various cellars and hiding places and gathered round, drawn by the sound of voices, and the old man appealed to them. Immediately a vociferous argument began, some maintaining that he was correct, others supporting the old woman. One thing emerged clearly. If the family had left, no one knew where they had intended going.

The captain raised his voice above the hubbub. 'We won't get any sense out of these people. If you ask me the shelling has driven them all mad.' He rode closer to Leo. 'The old girl will tell you anything she thinks will please you. She's hoping for a reward.'

Leo looked down at the old lady, who was clutching her stirrup and insisting on the truth of her assertion. 'Please! Are you telling the truth? Don't give me false hope.'

'I'm a mother and a grandmother,' she said. 'I know how it feels to lose a child. Your baby's safe somewhere. I wouldn't lie to you.'

'Thank you!' Leo felt in her pocket and took out some coins. 'I don't know if there is anything left to spend money on, but take these anyway. And thank you again.'

The captain gave a brief, contemptuous laugh and called his men to order. As they rode away Leo could see the old couple still arguing. She rode in silence, struggling to reconcile the chaos in her emotions, until she felt Victoria's hand on her arm.

'I'm so sorry, my dear. It's a cruel disappointment.'

Leo voiced the thoughts that were uppermost in her mind. 'If the family went north, then they are still in occupied territory. So there's no hope of finding them until the army pushes further forward. Perhaps not until the country has been liberated completely.'

'How could you trace them, even then?' Luke said. 'Needles and haystacks don't come close.'

'There must be ways,' Leo said. 'There must be refugee camps. Someone must be keeping some kind of records. Or maybe when the country is at peace they will come home to Lavci.'

Neither of her friends replied and they rode on in silence. By the time they reached Bitola Leo had come to a decision. She waited until they were back in the hospital, in the small, draughty room that served as a dining and sitting room for the staff. Then she said, 'Listen. There's obviously no chance of finding Alexandra until the war is over – or at least until the allies are in charge of most of the country. That could be this summer, but it might take longer. We've had so many false hopes raised about how long it will be before peace comes that I'm not going to rely on anything. I haven't decided whether to stay here or go home and wait, but I'm quite clear about one thing: I can't expect you two to hang around indefinitely. You have your own lives to lead, and Luke needs to get home to his children. I want you to go, as soon as you can find a ship to take you. And when I've found Alexandra – or when I'm sure that there is no point in going on looking – I'll come and visit you. That's my promise, and that's as far ahead as I can see. So please don't argue, or feel you can't leave me. I'm among friends here if I decide to stay on. If not, I shall go home to Tom. I'll miss you, of course I will. But it won't make life any easier for me if I am feeling guilty about you two. Do you understand?'

Luke and Victoria looked at each other. Then Luke took both Leo's hands in his. 'You are the bravest girl I know and I admire you more than I can say. But you are right. I need to get home and I want Victoria with me. Thank you.'

They left with a convoy the next morning and Leo travelled

with them to Salonika. Before she set off she spent a few minutes alone with Pierre Leseaux.

'I will be back, Pierre. But I don't know when. I'm going to see Luke and Victoria off and then I'm going to see General Bojovic to try to find out how he thinks the war is going. After that, I'll make a decision about whether to go back to England and wait or to come back here and help you. If there seems to be a chance of a quick victory, I'll stay here. If not . . .'

'If not you should go home,' he said. 'This uncertainty is taking its toll on you, I can see that. You should go home and find a life for yourself there. Then, if you find your little girl one day, you will have a home to take her back to. And if not . . .'

He left the sentence unfinished and Leo nodded. 'I understand. And you are right. Goodbye, Pierre. And thank you.'

'You should not be thanking me. It is the other way round. *Au revoir, ma petite, et bonne chance.*'

Seventeen

As soon as the three friends reached Salonika Luke went down to the docks to investigate the possibility of finding a ship that would take him and Victoria at least part of the way towards New Zealand. He returned with the news that a cargo vessel was leaving for Alexandria in two days' time and he had arranged with the captain to take them on board.

'Once we get to Alex,' he said, 'there shouldn't be a problem finding a ship to take us through the Suez Canal, maybe as far as Singapore. We might even manage to wangle our way on to a troop ship heading for Australia, or better still for Wellington.'

'The day after tomorrow!' Victoria turned to Leo. 'Now it's so close I don't know if I can bear to leave you here on your own.'

'Don't be silly!' Leo said. She could have wept at the prospect of losing her friends but she had made up her mind to do nothing to delay them. 'There's no point in you hanging around. Who knows when you might find another ship to take you?'

'I wish we knew for sure what you plan to do,' Luke said. 'I think we should both feel easier in our minds if we knew you were going home too.'

'It would be for the best, surely,' Victoria urged her. 'There's nothing you can do here and what about Tom? He must be longing to have you back.'

Leo nodded. 'Yes, you're probably right. He needs me, and there's not much point in my searching for the Popovics in the middle of the fighting. The sensible thing is for me to go home and wait.'

As she spoke she knew that it was the sensible decision, but the thought of leaving Salonika again dragged at her heart. She had arrived with such high hopes and she had a terrible premonition that if she once went back to England she might never return. A small, treacherous voice somewhere in her head was telling her to go home, marry Tom and abandon the fruitless search for her daughter.

'Do that!' Victoria said. 'It's much the best idea. Why doesn't Luke go back to the docks and see if there's a ship that will take you to Italy or Marseilles?'

'There's no need,' she protested. 'I'm quite capable of doing it for myself.'

In the event, all three of them went, only to discover that the only ships leaving for either destination in the immediate future were tramp steamers with no accommodation for a passenger.

'It doesn't matter,' Leo said. 'I can take the train to Athens. I'm bound to find something suitable there.'

The following day Leo went to call on her old friend General Bojovic, but was informed that he was no longer in Salonika. He had resigned after a disagreement with the High Command over the expansion of the Salonika front. Command was now in the hands of the Vovodja – the Serbian equivalent of Field Marshal – Duke Zivojin Miscic, a veteran of both Balkan Wars and the victor of several famous battles in the time before the Serbs were finally driven out of their homeland.

Indeed, there were those who said if he had been allowed to stand and fight, as he had wished, the terrible retreat through the mountains might never have happened. There had been changes at the head of the French army, too, which was now commanded by General Franchet D'Esperey – known to the English as Desperate Frankie. Leo sensed that there was a new sense of purpose in the air. On the way into the city they had passed gangs of workmen improving the roads that led to the mountains or making new ones, and railway lines were being laid. At last, it seemed, there was a real intention to sustain a new campaign until it resulted in victory.

Her next call was at the British consulate, to let them know she was back and to pick up any mail that had arrived in her absence. She had had dealings with the consul on various occasions and had the impression that he thoroughly disapproved of her, though he was always meticulously courteous. It was an attitude she was familiar with among men of his class and it did not bother her. There were not many letters, since very few of her acquaintances knew where she was. There was one from James Bartlett, her estate manager at Bramwell, to say that all was well and, in spite of the difficulties occasioned by lack of manpower and of horses, the harvest looked promising. There was another from her solicitors regarding minor repairs to the house in Sussex Gardens, and there were three from Tom. She kept those to read when she had dealt with the others. He seemed cheerful. The move to London had suited him very well and he found Sussex Gardens a congenial place to work; Sim and Beavis seemed to get on all right and made sure that he was well looked after; he was painting every day and the gallery owner who had been going to show his earlier work until it went up in smoke was interested in a new exhibition. He added that he missed Leo very much and hoped that she would come home in time to see it. *I hope every day to hear that you have found your daughter and are on your way back to London. Until that happens I shall not be able to fully enjoy all the other advantages which you have so generously provided for me. With all my love, Tom.*

Back at the hotel, Leo tried to compose a response, but she was so undecided about her future plans that she gave it up. She would write when Victoria and Luke had gone. She would have to make up her mind then.

She passed the rest of the day wandering the streets with her friends. Victoria was intent on finding the places she remembered from their first visit in 1912 but very little remained that was recognizable and, while it was a disappointment to her, it was a relief to Leo. She had no wish to be reminded of that more recent summer when she had returned with Sasha. All in all it was an unsatisfactory day for all of them. The awareness of their impending separation weighed on their spirits. Luke and Victoria were torn between anticipation of the new life ahead of them and their anxiety about leaving Leo, and she was struggling with the effort of remaining cheerful and positive in face of the prospect of being left alone.

As they ate their last dinner a thought suddenly came to Leo. 'You're going to get married. But you are not, yet. Won't that be a problem?'

'We've talked about it,' Luke said. 'I was all for waiting till we got back home. I reckoned turning up with a ready-made bride for the second time might be a bit much for my mother. But now I realize that it could cause all sorts of trouble. We're going to ask the ship's captain to marry us.'

Leo felt a lump rise in her throat. 'I wish I could be there. I should love to see you married.'

Victoria caught her hand. 'So do I, darling! Of all the people in the world I would want you at my wedding. We did think about tying the knot sooner, when you first came out here. But then we thought it would be better to wait until you had your little girl with you. But now . . .' Her words trailed off into silence.

Luke got up abruptly. 'I've had an idea. You two stay here and finish your meal. I'll see you back at the hotel in about an hour.'

He was gone before they could ask questions and was back sooner than he had promised, his eyes gleaming triumphantly. 'I've had a word with the chaplain at the British HQ. He'll marry us at eleven o'clock tomorrow morning on board that British destroyer in the harbour. Technically that's British soil, so he reckons it will be legal, but we can sort out any complications when we get to Wellington. Our ship doesn't sail till the afternoon tide, so we'll have plenty of time. How does that sound?'

Leo jumped up and kissed him. 'Luke, you're a genius! I'm so grateful.' She turned to her friend. 'Vita, this is all right with you, isn't it?'

Victoria put an arm round each of them. 'Of course it is. It's the best solution possible. Well done, Luke.'

'I'm afraid it won't be the sort of wedding you probably imagined for yourself,' he said ruefully. 'But then, it was never going to be.'

Victoria cocked an eyebrow ironically. 'My dear man, I never imagined any sort of wedding for myself. I was going to be fiercely independent all my life. You have completely shattered a young girl's dream!'

He hugged her. 'Well, all I can say is, I've managed to prevent a terrible waste of talent and beauty.'

It certainly was far from a conventional wedding. Victoria and Leo wore their travelling clothes, the only smart ones they had with them, and Luke was in tweeds. Victoria's bouquet was a branch of orange blossom which Luke snipped off a tree overhanging a garden wall on their way to the harbour. Leo acted as one witness and the ship's captain offered himself as the second. Leo had to keep a tight rein on her emotions. She sensed that if she once let go she would break down completely. She told herself over and over again that this was the ideal conclusion for both her friends, after six turbulent years, and she must be happy for them.

The captain entertained them to lunch after the ceremony and Leo was grateful for company to fill the time before the final parting. She sensed that the other two felt the same. In the end, they had to rush back to the hotel for their bags and then down to the harbour again where the newly-weds were just in time to board their ship before it sailed. At the foot of the gangway they exchanged long hugs.

Victoria was in tears. 'I wish we weren't going! We should have stayed. I can't bear the thought of leaving you all alone.'

'I'll be all right. You know me. I can cope with pretty well anything.'

'But you will go back to England now, won't you? Promise me you will. There's no point in hanging round here waiting for the war to finish.'

'No, you're right.'

'So you will go home? And write as soon as you get there.'

'And you must write as soon as you get to Wellington.'

'I will. I'll write to the London address.'

'Yes, do that.'

Luke intervened. 'Sorry, girls. We have to get on board now. The skipper's making threatening gestures.' He took Leo's hands. 'Now, we expect to see you in New Zealand just as soon as you can make it – you and Tom, and little Alexandra. That's what we can all look forward to.'

Leo nodded wordlessly. She wanted them to go, before she finally lost control. He kissed her on the cheek and took Victoria by the hand to lead her up the gangway. Mercifully, the ship was ready to cast off, so Leo did not have to wait on the quayside very long. Her friends stood at the rail and waved and she waved back, until she lost sight of the ship among the other vessels crowding the harbour. Then she turned away and walked back towards the centre of town. She no longer wanted to weep. Instead she was filled with a terrible emptiness and a sudden sense of exhaustion.

She told herself she would feel better after a good night's sleep, but she woke the next morning possessed by the same weariness. She knew that she should make arrangements for going home, but she could not summon up the resolve to go to the station and enquire about trains to Athens. Instead, she wandered out of the town and eventually found herself sitting on a flat rock at a point along the shore where she could watch the coming and going of ships in the harbour. She wrestled with the decision facing her. Common sense told her that she should go back to England. After all, there was nothing to be gained from hanging around in Salonika, waiting for a new campaign which, on previous form, might never materialize. Even if it did, it could be months before the armies moved forward enough for her to begin her search. It would be far more sensible to go home and wait until the war was over and conditions had returned to something like normal. But how long might that take? She had promised Victoria that she would go. Or had she, actually? And Tom was waiting for her – but then, Tom seemed to be coping perfectly well without her. The thoughts went round and round in her head, without coming to any resolution. The point she came back to over and over again was the feeling that if she gave up now and went home she might never return. After all, she had never even seen her child, never held her in her arms. It would be easy to decide that it would be best all round to leave her with the family she had learned to regard as her own; easy to conclude that the chance of finding her was so slim that it was not worth taking. That temptation, that sense that she might betray her daughter, betray the one legacy Sasha had left her, was what kept her immobile on her rock until the sun was low on the horizon.

The next morning she was no nearer coming to a decision. She needed some kind of sign, some event that would prompt her in one direction or the other. All day she sat watching the ships, her mind almost blank, waiting. Then, late in the afternoon, she saw a ship flying the British flag sailing into the harbour. It was a cargo ship, probably bringing supplies for the garrison, and when it had unloaded it would, presumably, be heading back to England. Here was her sign! With any luck she would be able to buy a passage. It would be easier than travelling over land to Athens and then hoping to find a vessel to take her onwards. Leo got up and headed back into town, to the consulate, to make enquiries.

She had walked further than she realized and it took her almost an hour to get there. The consul greeted her with his usual formal politeness.

'Ah, Miss Malham Brown! You saw the ship coming in, no doubt, and are here to collect your mail. There was no need for you to trouble yourself. I was about to have it brought up to your hotel.' He took a small package from his desk and held it out to her. 'Not many letters this time, I'm afraid.'

Leo explained the principal reason for her visit and the consul agreed to make enquiries about getting a passage for her on the ship's return journey.

'Very wise of you, if I may say so!'

She took the packet of letters to a nearby café, ordered a *citron pressé* and unsealed the outer envelope. As the consul had said, the contents were sparse. There was a letter from a firm of solicitors whose name seemed vaguely familiar and another addressed in a handwriting she did not recognize. She opened this one first and withdrew a sheet of paper with a black border.

> *Dear Miss Leonora,*
>
> *I hope you will forgive my presumption in writing to you, but I did not want you to receive this news from strangers. Sir Thomas died yesterday, June 2nd, at about four o'clock in the morning. He caught this new kind of flu that is going round and went downhill very quickly. The doctors said his experiences in the trenches had sapped his strength and being confined to a wheelchair had weakened his lungs. They did everything they could for him and I don't think he suffered too much. I know his solicitors will be writing to you but I am hoping that you may read this letter first.*
>
> *He was conscious and quite clear in his mind until the very last and he wanted me to give you a message. He said to tell you that he loved you as the best friend a man could ever have and if things had been different he would have loved you as a husband and he was sorry that that could never have been. He said you would understand what he meant.*
>
> *He also made a new will and asked me to witness it, along with the doctor. First, I should tell you that he had a very successful exhibition at the Albermarle gallery and sold almost all his paintings, except for six which he would not part with because they meant too much to him. Five of these he has left to you, along with some other keepsakes. The sixth, kind and generous employer that he was, he gave to me. It's not one of the wartime ones. We'd both seen enough of the trenches. It's the one he painted last autumn of the Hall, with all the trees in their brilliant colours. I shall always treasure it as a reminder*

of these last few happy months. It isn't his only generous gift. He has left me a little nest egg, enough to set myself up in a country pub, which is what I have always fancied.

I know this will be a terrible shock to you and I wish I didn't have to give you such bad news. You and Sir Thomas were very good to me and made me feel like part of the family and not just a servant. I shall always be grateful. I hope you have found your little girl and will be home soon. If you want to contact me, you know my mother's address. I shall be there for the time being and shall hope to hear from you.
Respectfully yours,
Arnold Simkins (Sim)

The solicitors' letter repeated the same information in more legalistic terms. Leo folded both letters carefully and replaced them in their envelopes. She did not weep. Tears were pointless now. With Tom's death the last shred of her old life had been ripped away and there was nothing to go home for. She had the sign she was waiting for. She got up and set off for the Red Cross hospital, where she volunteered her services on the condition that she be sent back to Bitola, to work with Pierre Leseaux.

Eighteen

In a prisoner-of-war camp close to the Bulgarian border four Serbian soldiers crouched in the shade of a hut. One of them was older than the others, a grizzled veteran with sunken eyes. Next to him was a younger man but both, from their emaciated faces and ragged clothes, had obviously been prisoners for a long time. The third man was younger still, hardly more than a boy, and in better shape, lacking the air of dull resignation which the others wore. The fourth man sat a little apart, his arms clasped round his knees, his face almost completely hidden by a tangled mass of hair and beard, from among which dark eyes watched his companions without expression.

'So how long have you two been here?' the boy asked.

The oldest man spat into the dust. 'Too bloody long! Since the beginning of 'seventeen.'

The newcomer grimaced. 'Eighteen months in this hellhole!' He looked at the second man. 'How about you?'

'Not much less. They picked me up when we had to retreat from Lavci.'

'Lavci? That name rings a bell. Wasn't that where Colonel Malkovic bought it?'

'That's how they got me,' the veteran said. 'I was one of the ones who went out to try to bring back his body. No hope! The Bulgars were all over us. The other three with me were all killed.'

The boy hunched his shoulders. 'Three dead and you captured. Was it worth it to bring back a dead body?'

The older man looked at him with something approaching contempt. 'You obviously never served under the colonel, or you wouldn't ask that.'

'No. I only joined up three months ago. My family evacuated to Athens when the war started. I wanted to volunteer then but they said I was too young. I went to Salonika and joined up as soon as I was seventeen.'

'In that case I suppose you can be forgiven. If you'd known the colonel you'd understand.'

'He was a good officer, then?'

'The best. Any one of us would have gladly died for him. Isn't that so, Goran?'

'Absolutely. He brought us through the Albanian mountains in 'fifteen and stayed with us in Corfu, made sure we were looked after. Always made sure we had a share of whatever food was going before he touched a mouthful himself. That's the sort of officer he was.'

'Not many like him,' the boy said.

'You can say that again!'

'Funny, though,' the boy went on, 'there were some weird stories going round the barracks about him.'

'What do you mean, weird?'

'Something about some English tart claiming he'd fathered a child on her. Not the sort of thing . . .'

A feral howl cut him short. The fourth man launched himself at the boy, his fingers clutching for his throat. The other two grabbed him and pulled him off.

'All right, Slobo, all right!' The old man spoke soothingly, as if to a child. 'Calm down. The boy doesn't understand, that's all.'

The man addressed as Slobo withdrew unwillingly to his former position and sat, glowering.

Goran said, 'You'd better be careful how you speak about the Lady Leonora, or Slobo won't be the only one you offend. She was the bravest, kindest lady I've ever come across. She came out in 'fifteen to nurse our men and she was with us all through that terrible retreat through the mountains. When I copped a bullet in the shoulder from some bastard of an Albanian bandit she dressed it for me. And she stayed with us all the time in Corfu. We reckoned it was her, even more than the colonel, that organized food supplies and firewood when we first arrived. We all knew what was going on between them. It was a bit irregular but we didn't care. She and the colonel were made for each other. So don't ever call her a tart again.'

'You don't know the half of it,' the old man said. 'She was there in 1912, when we kicked out the Turks. I remember her at Adrianople, nursing typhus patients. There're a lot of men alive today who'd be underground if it wasn't for her.'

The boy squirmed and ducked his head. 'I'm sorry. I didn't mean any disrespect. I was only repeating what I heard from some of the old hands.'

'Not anyone who's ever known her, or the colonel,' Goran said. 'That's for certain.'

The boy looked uneasily at the fourth man. 'What's up with him? He doesn't say much, does he?'

'Old Slobodan? Take no notice of him. He's had a bad time. When he got here he hardly knew his own name.' Goran turned his head away and made a gesture of screwing his finger into his temple. 'Shell shock, if you ask me.'

There was a brief silence, then the old man said, 'You've only been in three months? Blimey, you didn't last long, did you? Where did they get you?'

'In the foothills of the Sar. I volunteered for forward reconnaissance. We walked straight into a Bulgarian patrol.'

Goran leaned forward quickly. 'The Sar? What in God's name were you doing there?'

'General Miscic's orders. It's the start of a new campaign.'

'In the Sar mountains? Miscic must have gone mad! The Bulgars have held those peaks since they invaded. An assault from there would be suicide. There's only one way to Skopje and then on to Belgrade and that's along the Vardar valley.'

The boy shrugged. 'I heard the British and the Greeks were preparing to attack that way.'

'That's typical!' the old man snarled. 'We've been shafted again. The Brits and the Greeks are going to stroll up the Vardar and take all the glory while our men kill themselves trying to dislodge the Bulgars from Mount Veternik.'

'Maybe it's just a diversion,' Goran said. 'A ploy to get the Bulgars to move troops from the Vardar to the Sar.'

'Let's hope so!' the old man said. 'No one in his right mind could really expect to break through on that front.'

'Unless . . .' Slobodan's word was hardly more than a murmur and the others took no notice.

The old man smiled for the first time. 'It's true, then! At last! There is a new campaign.'

'Oh, yes. And this time nothing is going to stop us. Men were saying we'd be back in Belgrade by Christmas.'

'God! I'd like to be there to see that!' Goran muttered. 'There must be a way out of this place. Once our men are in Skopje we might be able to link up with them. What do you think, Jorge?'

The old man shook his head. 'I've survived this long. I want to see my home again. I'm not taking any risks at this stage.'

They were silent for a time. At length the boy said, 'What happened to her – the English lady?'

Goran gave him a sardonic look. 'You didn't get the full story from your blabbermouthed friends then?'

'No, I suppose not. Why? What happened?'

Goran leaned closer. 'OK. Now what you are about to hear is from the horse's mouth, not just gossip. "Cos I was there, see? I was in Lavci when it happened.'

'When what happened?'

'You're right about the colonel getting a child on her. That night, the night he died, she came to Lavci. She was nursing in the hospital at Bitola and when she heard he'd been wounded she came straight there. Never mind it was winter, and the middle of a battle zone and she was pretty far gone with the child. She thought he needed her and she came. That's the sort of woman she was. ''Course, she didn't know it was no good, that he'd been left for dead on the battlefield. When she heard, she went into labour with the shock of it.'

'And . . .?'

'Well, what do you expect? No one in Bitola has been getting enough to eat, her included. What with that and the shock, she didn't stand a chance, poor lady.'

'So she died?'

'And the child with her,' Jorge said grimly. He crossed himself. 'God rest her soul – and the kid's, whatever it was.'

Goran turned to him. 'No! You're wrong there, Jorge. You weren't around at the end. You'd gone off to try and bring the colonel's body back. The kid survived. I know, because the doc had us out scouring the village for a woman who'd recently had a child, to be a wet nurse for it.'

'Did they find anyone?'

'Yes. I saw her being taken into the house where the colonel had set up his HQ. I asked one of the locals who she was. What was the name now?' He wrinkled his brow. 'Pop-something. Popovic, that's it.'

He stopped speaking abruptly, at a sudden movement from Slobodan. For a moment it looked as if he might launch himself at one of them again, then he sank back and resumed his former position. But his eyes were no longer vacant.

'I wonder where the kid is now,' the boy mused.

'God alone knows,' Goran said. 'We had to pull out of Lavci the next day and the Bulgars moved back in. Last I saw the place was being shelled to blazes. The family may have survived, but the chances are pretty slim.'

'Pity, that,' Jorge said. 'Sad to think the colonel left no one to carry on his name.'

'Come to think of it, it's not just a name, is it?' Goran's tone was suddenly more animated. 'He was an aristocrat – Count Alexander Malkovic. There must be an estate as well as a title. And that kid is the only heir.'

'Not a legitimate heir,' the boy objected. 'I mean, when all's said and done, he and this English lady weren't married, were they?'

'No, they weren't,' Jorge agreed. 'The colonel had a wife, a Serbian lady, but I don't think there were any children. I seem to remember hearing that he sent her off to Athens for safety when the war started and he wouldn't have had a chance to see her since. But I can't believe she'd be prepared to recognize his bastard as a legitimate heir.'

'Why not?' Goran pursued. 'If they want to keep the estate in the family, this kid is their only chance. I reckon there are probably men out searching for him – or her – right now.'

'Well, I don't give much for their chances of finding him,' Jorge said with a shrug.

'Maybe not,' his friend agreed. 'They wouldn't know where to start. How many people were around when it happened? Only the men of our company, and the locals of course, and most of them are probably dead. But for someone who knew who to look for . . .'

Jorge gave a brief laugh. 'Goran, you're a dreamer! You're a POW, remember? And even if you weren't . . .'

'Just imagine, though,' Goran said. 'I reckon anyone who could find that kid and hand it over to the colonel's family would be made for life. It's got to be worth a nice little pension, maybe a bit of land on the estate, or a job with the family . . . And if the war is nearly over, we won't be POWs for much longer.'

A bugle sounded on the far side of the camp. Jorge hauled himself to his feet. 'Come on, that's dinner. Let's get to the cookhouse while there's still something left to eat.'

The others rose and followed him, the man they called Slobodan a short distance behind. None of them looked back to see that the eyes that peered out from the tangle of hair now glittered with purpose.

★   ★   ★

'*Mon dieu!* It's not possible!' Pierre Leseaux craned his neck to gaze up at the towering rampart of mountains that stretched north and south in front of him. Precipitous slopes gave way to sheer cliffs and above all floated the snowy peaks, some of them 8000 foot above sea level.

Standing beside him, Leo shivered involuntarily, although where they were in the foothills the September sun was still warm. The thought of anyone attempting to scale those crags, even unopposed, made her stomach churn.

'And the Bulgars are entrenched up there?' she asked.

The young lieutenant acting as their guide nodded soberly. 'Their front line runs along the crest. The spotter planes have brought back photographs of the blockhouses they've built. We are relying on our artillery to smash them before we advance.'

'*Pouffe!*' Leseaux gave vent to a French expression of disbelief. 'You will never get artillery up there.'

The lieutenant grinned for the first time. 'You think not? Already we have 155mm and 105mm guns halfway up. When we get them to the top they will dominate the Bulgarian positions.'

'Halfway up?' Leseaux scanned the mountainside. 'I can't see anything.'

'Exactly! Nor can the enemy planes, we hope. The guns are moved at night and every day they are camouflaged. When they finally open up it will take the Bulgars completely by surprise.'

'At night!' Leo said. 'But how?'

'They are hauled up by tractors and cranes.'

Leseaux shook his head. 'I would never have believed it possible.'

'No,' the young man agreed soberly. 'Nor would I. But General Miscic saw that it could be done and he convinced General d'Espery – and the miracle is happening. But it is the men who are making it happen. They are working like slaves and nothing is allowed to stand in their way.' He smiled. 'We are going home, you see.'

'But surely,' Leseaux said, 'this is just a diversionary attack. The real advance will be along the Vardar valley.'

'That is what the Bulgars will expect,' the lieutenant agreed. 'We are going to show them different.'

The Serbs, with their French allies, had moved forward from Bitola over the summer and Pierre Leseaux and his field hospital had followed. Leo had taken up her old duties as a nurse, but it was understood between them that at every new village or farm she would be free to pursue her quest for information. She had knocked on doors and stopped women in the street or old men working in the fields with the same questions. 'Have any refugees passed through here?' 'Do you know anyone called Popovic?' It was not an uncommon name and more than once she had arrived at a cottage with her heart beating fast and her stomach quivering with anticipation, only to be met with blank incomprehension. Every time she saw a woman with a little girl of the right age she had to quell the impulse to rush up to her and demand to know if the child was her own or was left with her by a stranger. As the army moved west towards the mountains she became increasingly frustrated. She had begged to be allowed to rejoin Leseaux because he understood her situation and had proved a good friend, but now she began to think that she should instead have applied to the British Red Cross, who were with the British contingent in the Vardar area. If the Popovic family had survived and fled north it was almost certain that they would have taken that route. The likelihood of finding them here in these inhospitable mountains was remote in the extreme. However, loyalty to Leseaux and her colleagues prevented her from leaving and she could only hope that when the breakthrough finally came, if it ever did, she would be able to follow in the wake of the victorious forces.

The field hospital had been set up in a collection of tents in a steep sided valley. As yet, they had few casualties to deal with, but many of the beds were already occupied. There were still cases of malaria but the main enemy now was the Spanish flu, which had infected their ranks just as it had swept across most of Europe. It was the very disease that had killed Tom and nursing the victims was a constant reminder to Leo of her loss.

One evening she persuaded the lieutenant to take her to

see the guns being moved up the mountainside. They rode up to the head of the valley and then followed a rough track that zigzagged higher and higher up the slopes of the mountain.

'This was just a goat track a couple of months ago,' her guide told her. 'Now you see what has been achieved.'

Trees had been felled to widen the path and their trunks used to bridge streams and gullies. The surface of the ground was already worn into deep ruts by the passing of heavy vehicles and they overtook a steady stream of mules and men on foot, carrying supplies and equipment. As they climbed further Leo became aware of the sound of engines and shouted orders and a low, rhythmic murmur which resolved itself as they got closer into the sound of men's voices united in effort. At length, the track opened out on to a narrow plateau at the foot of a sheer cliff and to a scene that reminded Leo of a canvas by Breugel. In the light of naphtha flares teams of men hauled on ropes which disappeared into the darkness of the night sky. Craning her neck, she could just make out the shapes of huge timber derricks perched on the edge of the cliff and halfway up a field gun swayed and jerked as the men hauled. At the foot of the cliff, two more guns waited to be lifted in their turn.

Leo turned to her companion. 'It's incredible! But is that the top? Where do they go from there?'

'It's very far from the top,' he said. 'Beyond the plateau there is another track which has been blasted into the side of the mountain. The guns are hauled up by tractors and there are several more places where they have to be lifted like this. But the work is nearly finished. These are the last few guns. In a day or two we shall be ready to launch the attack.'

He was correct in his estimate, but when the last gun was in place days passed while the whole army waited tensely for the order.

'What are the generals waiting for?' was the question on everyone's lips but no one knew the answer. Somewhere, higher up the chain of command that stretched back to Paris, there was hesitation or uncertainty. Then, on the fourteenth of September, Leo was woken by the roar of gunfire which echoed and ricocheted around the mountains. All day the barrage continued, deafening in its intensity. Unit after unit of infantry marched out of camp, heading up the narrow valleys towards the crest of the ridge they called Dobro Polje and Leo and her colleagues prepared for the inevitable casualties. At nightfall the guns fell silent but before dawn they heard new sounds from above. This time it was the crackle of small arms fire. Wounded began to trickle back, but not in the numbers they had anticipated, and they told of a steady advance against less determined opposition than expected. Then, in the afternoon, a messenger arrived in the camp to announce triumphantly that the Serbs had taken Mount Veternik. By nightfall, Mount Sokol had also been conquered. The Serbian and French forces now dominated the Belgian front line.

From that moment on the Serbian advance was unstoppable. All night they pushed forward, the Bulgarian defence crumbling before them. By the following day they had taken the Kozyak Ridge, six miles further north. Here they encountered more determined resistance from a German battalion, which had been rushed forward to bolster the Bulgarian lines, but nothing was going to stand in the way of the Serbian troops now. For three days they advanced without pausing to rest or eat, carrying nothing with them except ammunition. The Bulgarians, starved of supplies and demoralized by rumours of riots and dissension at home, took to their heels. On the twenty-first British spotter planes reported seeing the mountain defile west of Robrovo jammed with retreating Bulgarians. By September twenty-sixth the road to Skopje was wide open, though the town itself remained in enemy hands, and beyond that lay the main route to Belgrade.

Pierre Leseaux's field hospital followed the advancing troops. In Tetovo, where they took over the local hospital, Leo resumed her perpetual search. She began at the town hall where, at first, she was met with the usual blank faces and shaken heads. In the chaos of war floods of displaced people had swept back and forth around the country and local officials had long ago given up any attempt to keep records. Eventually, however, the mayor reluctantly admitted that a camp had been set up for

refugees a mile or two outside the town. Leo rode out immediately but with little hope that her enquiries would bear fruit.
When she reached the place she almost found herself hoping
that the Popovics had not come here. It was a bleak cluster of
makeshift hovels, constructed out of tree branches and roughly
thatched with bracken. There had been rain recently, and the
paths between them had been churned into mud and there
was, as far as Leo could see, no attempt at proper sanitation.

She tethered her horse and began her eternal repetition of
the same questions. Most of the occupants of the camp were
women, many with young children. The only men were those
who were too old for military service. Sometimes she was
greeted with sympathetic interest, more often with suspicion,
occasionally with a silent shrug and averted faces. Then a
woman crouching over a small fire said, 'Popovic? A family
with a baby girl? There was a woman I met a while back
when I went down to the stream to fetch water. She had a
little mite with her. I remember because the child had red hair
– well, not red exactly. More the colour of yours. I think she
said her name was Popovic.'

'Where?' Leo gasped the word. 'Do you know where I can
find them?'

'I'm not sure. Not just round here, anyway. I know most
of the people in this part of the camp. I suppose she must have
come from over the other side somewhere. But it was sometime
ago. A month, maybe. They may have moved on by now.'

Breathlessly Leo thanked her and stumbled away through
the mud towards the far side of the camp. But here she met
with no greater success than before. No one seemed to
remember a family with a red-haired child or, if they did, they
thought it better to pretend ignorance.

Then a young woman sitting in front of a tepee of branches
suckling a baby called her over. 'You're looking for the Popovic
family?'

'Yes! Do you know them?'

'They were living there,' she indicated the collapsed remains
of a hut. 'But they moved on some time ago – must be a
month or more.'

'Do you know where they went?'

'The father had a cousin in Skopje, I think. They were trying to get there.'

'In Skopje?' Leo struggled to order her thoughts. At last, in this most unexpected place, she had found a definite lead. But if the Popovics were in Skopje, how could she hope to trace them, in a city that size? At least it was confirmation that they had survived until a month ago, and that her daughter was still alive – if indeed this child was her daughter. 'And they had a little girl with them – a child with hair the same colour as mine?'

The woman regarded her curiously. 'Yes, now you come to mention it. Why are you looking for them?'

Leo squatted on the ground beside her, suddenly overcome. 'If it is the family I am looking for, then the child is mine. She was given to them to care for because I was too ill to look after her myself, and I've been searching for her ever since.'

The tears which she had been suppressing for many long days filled her eyes and overflowed down her cheeks and the other woman reached out and laid a hand on her arm. 'These are terrible times. We all know what it is like to lose a child. My eldest son was killed when a shell hit our home. And now this little one is sick and I do not know what to do for him.'

Leo raised her head and rubbed her hand across her cheek. 'Let me see? I am a nurse. I may be able to help.'

It was obvious at a glance that the child was severely malnourished. 'You are feeding him yourself?'

The woman sighed. 'I try. But I have hardly any milk. There is no food to be had anywhere.'

'No food? But there is food in the shops in town. I saw it myself.'

'Oh, for the locals, yes. But they won't sell it to us. They say they have only enough for themselves – and anyway, they don't want us here. I think they hope that if they starve us we will go away.'

Leo hauled herself to her feet. 'That is criminal! It's unforgivable and it has got to be stopped.'

She looked down at the woman, feeling a sudden excess of

new energy. 'Don't worry. I am going to get this put right. You and your child shall be fed – and the rest of the people here, too.'

The woman caught the hem of her skirt. 'Bless you! But can you do this? Can you really help?'

Leo nodded grimly. 'Oh, yes. I've learned from experience that there are always ways of making people understand what their duty is. I shall be back before evening, I promise.'

As she turned away the woman clutched her skirt again. 'The family you are looking for – the man said his cousin was a blacksmith. Perhaps that might help you to find them.'

As she strode back through the camp Leo became aware for the first time of the signs of malnutrition and disease among the many children who grovelled in the mud or stood listlessly gazing as she passed. She collected her horse and rode back to the hospital as fast as she could. There, she went straight to the small room Leseaux had taken over for an office. Half an hour later she and the doctor confronted a very flustered mayor, and when he tried to make excuses Leseaux suggested smoothly that perhaps General Miscic, who had set up a temporary headquarters a few miles further on, should be informed of the problem. He was sure that the general would be very distressed by the thought that Serbs were treating their fellow countrymen so heartlessly. As the sun began to dip towards the horizon, Leo led a small cavalcade into the refugee camp. Behind her came a wagon filled with provisions 'donated' by shop keepers in the town and a group of nurses equipped with medicines and inoculations for typhoid and smallpox. They set up a small tent and before long a queue of mothers carrying or dragging small children had formed in front of it. Leo herself headed straight for the tepee where she had met the woman who had given her the first news of her daughter. She carried a flask of milk, a loaf of bread, a sausage and two apples.

'It's not much but it will strengthen you, and from now on you should be able to buy food in the town. Do you have money?'

'Very little.'

Leo reached into her pocket and handed over a purse. The woman tried to refuse it but Leo pressed it into her hand.

'Believe me, you have given me hope when I had almost given up. That is worth far more than the money in this purse.'

It was dark by the time they were able to pack up their equipment and head back to the hospital. It comforted Leo to think that they had undoubtedly saved lives here, but along with that thought came the recognition that there must be hundreds of other women and children in similar conditions all over the country. In the face of that fact her own single-minded quest for her daughter seemed selfish.

The following day, September the twenty-eighth, news came that the Spahis, the French-Moroccan cavalry, had stormed into Skopje and driven out the occupying German troops.

The field hospital followed a day later and set up camp on the outskirts of the town. The fighting was over for the moment but they still had plenty of patients: men who had walked and fought for days and nights until they collapsed from exhaustion or the effect of untreated wounds; and, increasingly, those who had succumbed to flu. As soon as she felt she could be spared, Leo went to Pierre Leseaux and told him what she had learned in Tetovo. He immediately insisted that she should take all the time she needed to follow up this lead.

'A truck is going into Skopje to collect supplies in half an hour. You can get a lift on that. God grant that this time you may be lucky!'

Once there she began, as usual, at the town hall, where she found a scene of chaos as a throng of people besieged the officials, demanding ration cards or attempting to trace friends and relatives. After a long wait she persuaded a harassed clerk to let her see the register of local residents. There were a number of Popovics but the list also gave details of their occupations, and a short way through it she gave a cry of triumph. There was a Popovic whose trade was given as a blacksmith. She scanned the rest of the list in case there was more than one but found no one else. This, surely, must be the cousin with whom the family she was looking for had hoped to take refuge!

The address given was in a suburb on the far side of the city and Leo's first flush of excitement was dampened by the realization that getting there was not going to be easy. The retreating Germans had blown up the bridge over the River Vardar, making travel around the city extremely difficult. She had no vehicle of her own and in the general chaos public transport had pretty well ceased to operate. Requests for a taxi or a hire car were met with ironic laughter and shaken heads. After many enquiries and a long wait she managed to squeeze on to one of the few buses that were running, which took her to within two miles of her destination, but from there she had no option but to walk. Normally she would have thought nothing of it but that morning she had woken with a headache and the beginnings of a sore throat. She had pushed the sensation to the back of her mind but now, as she trudged along the unfamiliar street, she became aware that she was running a fever. It was not an unfamiliar sensation. From her early experiences in Adrianople, through the cold and wet of Lamarck, the FANY hospital in Calais, and on to Kragujevac, where she had worked under Mabel Stobart in the early years of the war, she had grown used, like all the nurses, to working with a minor infection of some sort. Normally she could shrug it off, but today she found herself tiring much more quickly and all her muscles began to ache.

She reached the place at last and was greeted by the sounds and smells that were familiar to her from any army camp or from her own home village of Bramwell: the hiss of hot metal being quenched in water; the ring of hammer on anvil and the smell of scorching hoof. She skirted the blacksmith's yard and walked up to the door of the small house beside it. Her heart was pounding. In her imagination she saw the door being opened by a rosy-cheeked woman with a small, red-headed child clinging to her skirts. She did not doubt for one moment that she would recognize her instantly.

The door was opened, not by a woman, but by a scrawny boy with a pinched, suspicious face.

Leo had to make an effort to collect her thoughts. 'Good

day. I'm looking for a Mrs Popovic, but not the lady who lives here. Do you have some relations from Lavci staying with you?'

The boy stared at her for a moment, then backed away and disappeared through a door at the rear of the house. Leo heard voices and then the door reopened and a woman came towards her. She was not the full-breasted, motherly figure of her imagination, but thin and grey-haired with a worn, lined face.

'Who are you?' she demanded. 'What do you want?'

'My name is Leonora Malham Brown.'

It was clear that the name meant nothing but Leo had the impression that the women was uncomfortable about something. She seemed to find it difficult to look Leo straight in the face, gazing either beyond her or down to the floor.

Leo went on: 'Am I right in thinking that you and your family are refugees from Lavci?'

In answer the woman shrugged and nodded, wordlessly implying the question, 'What business is it of yours?'

'Before you left there, a year ago last January, you agreed to take care of a baby girl. There was a battle going on. The mother had come to the village and gave birth prematurely but she was too ill to care for the child so she was given to you to nurse. That is right, isn't it?'

The woman's eyes flicked from left to right. 'Yes, I took the child in. The Serbian captain begged me. I couldn't let it die.'

'Of course not!' Leo said warmly. 'And it was a wonderful thing you did.' She hesitated, unable to think how to explain herself in the face of this blank defensiveness. 'Please, what is your first name?'

'Yelena. Why?'

'Yelena, I am the women who gave birth to that child. I am her mother, and I have been looking for her ever since. Please!' She reached out and seized the woman's care-roughened hands. 'Please, can I see her?'

The hands were pulled away and wrapped in the woman's apron, as if they might betray some secret. 'She's not here.'

'Not here?' After the peak of expectation Leo could hardly take in the words. 'Do you mean she is out somewhere – playing perhaps?'

'No. She's not here any more.'

'I don't understand.' Then an idea came to her, a possibility that gave a gleam of hope. Of course, Yelena Popovic had come to care for the child, to regard her perhaps as her own daughter. Probably she had been dreading just such a day as this. She stretched out her hand again. 'Yelena, I think I understand how you feel. You have children of your own, don't you?'

'Three.'

'And I know how you must love them. Alexandra is my only child. My . . . my husband was killed at Lavci. I have nothing, no one else. Please, let me have my daughter! I have come all the way from England to find her.'

Yelena stepped back. 'You are English?'

'Yes.'

'Then you are not the child's mother. She is the daughter of a great Serbian nobleman, a count.'

'Yes, Count Alexander Malkovic – but he is dead.'

'Alexandra has gone to be with her family. A man came to collect her.'

'What do you mean? What man?'

'He said his name was Slobodan and he had been sent by the Malkovic family to find the child. He has taken her to them.'

'When? When was this?'

'Not long ago. Eight, ten days.'

Leo felt her legs give way under her. She sagged against the doorpost, almost unable to breathe. 'You have given my child away to a stranger? God knows what he may have done with her! What proof did he give you that he came from the Malkovic family?'

'The child had a locket, left with her by the doctor who brought her into the world.'

'Yes! Yes!'

'The man was able to tell me what was inscribed inside it, so I knew he must be genuine.'

'But I am her mother!' Leo was sobbing now. 'She belongs to me, not to them! Where has he taken her? Where?'

Yelena Popovic shrugged. 'Belgrade, I suppose. That's what he said. I'm sorry. There's nothing I can do. Alexandra has gone to live with her real family. You will have to speak to them.'

'But how can I? Belgrade is still in enemy hands . . .' Her words were cut short by the slam of the door.

For a long time Leo stood propped against the doorpost, tears running down her face. Men passing by threw her curious looks and one muttered something about 'got her in the family way and then chucked her out, I shouldn't wonder'. Slowly she regained control and began to think. If the man knew what was inscribed in the locket, the family motto of the Malkovics, then he must have come from them, and the only person who could have sent him was Eudoxie, Sasha's wife. Somehow she must have heard about Alexandra's birth. That was not so surprising. Plenty of people had been around at the time and gossip had probably reached Eudoxie in Athens. Leo wondered what had happened to the new will he had mentioned in his last letter, in which he repudiated his marriage and declared her child as his heir. If that had been destroyed was it possible that Eudoxie might be prepared to pass Alexandra off as her own? She offered, after all, the only possible way of continuing the Malkovic line and much would depend on that in terms of money and land, once the occupying Bulgarians had been driven out. The child could have been born during her time of exile in Athens. No one would be any the wiser.

With an effort Leo straightened up and began the long walk back. The situation was becoming clear: Eudoxie had heard about the birth, and presumably been told the name of the foster mother, and she had sent out men to search, just as Leo herself had been searching. The bitter fact was that one of them had reached his target just before her own arrival. There was only one course of action open now. She must wait until Belgrade itself had fallen and the Bulgarians had finally been ousted. Then she would go to the Malkovic home and demand her child. The threat of a scandal should be enough to ensure her victory.

A chill wind was coming off the mountains and Leo found she was shivering. By the time she reached the bus stop the shivering had become convulsive, her head was burning and she felt faint. Mercifully a bus appeared quite quickly, but that only took her to the city centre. She still had to get back to the place where the hospital had set up camp. Only half aware of what she was doing she began to plod in that direction. A wave of dizziness swept over her and she caught at a lamppost for support. Then, somehow, she was sitting on the cold ground and darkness was closing in around her.

Nineteen

Leo regained partial consciousness to the sensation of being lifted and moved but then she lapsed back into oblivion. After that she was only aware of alternately burning with fever and shivering, of the unending ache in all her muscles and the pain in her head. Arms lifted her, cups were held to her lips, her face and neck were bathed with cool water but she hardly knew where she was or how she had got there. Then, one morning, she woke with the instinctive knowledge that the fever had left her. She was weak, so weak that she could hardly lift her head off the pillow, but the pain and the burning had gone. Gazing up at the ceiling she realized that she was no longer in one of the tented wards of the field hospital. She was in a private cubicle, but from the sounds she could hear from beyond the walls she guessed that it was part of a larger ward. She tried to remember what had happened just before she collapsed, but her last clear recollection was of hearing the triumphant news that Skopje had fallen.

It was a relief when the door opened to see a face she recognized. It was a young Irish nurse called Jeannie.

'God be praised, you're awake!' the girl exclaimed. 'How are you feeling?'

'Death warmed up – but only slightly.' Leo's mouth seemed reluctant to obey her and the words came out slurred.

'Well, that's not surprising. Let's see if we can make you more comfortable. Then I'll call Doctor Pierre. He'll be mightily relieved to hear you're on the mend. To be sure, there have been times in the last day or two when we thought we were going to lose you altogether.'

Leseaux came hurrying in soon afterwards. He looked at the chart at the end of her bed, felt her forehead and took her pulse and nodded. 'So, we are over the worst – or let us hope so. You have given us some very anxious moments, *ma petite*. But what happened? One of our drivers found you collapsed at the side of the road. Did you find the little one?'

'The little one?' Leo queried. Something was stirring in her memory but her brain seemed to be full of fog.

'Your daughter. You went to find her. Do you remember?'

It came back to her then, with the force of a physical blow, so that she whimpered with the pain of it. Leseaux took her hand in his. '*Ma chère* Leo! Forgive me. I did not mean to distress you. Can you tell me what happened?'

'Not there,' Leo mumbled. 'Taken away. A man took her away.'

'A man? What man?'

'I don't know. She said . . . the woman said he was taking her back to her family.'

She jerked up in the bed, so that Leseaux laid his hand on her shoulder to press her back, murmuring, 'Rest, rest. You must try to be still.'

'Belgrade!' Leo said. 'He has taken her to Belgrade. I have to go there!'

'You must be patient. You are far too weak to go anywhere and anyway our forces have not yet reached Belgrade. It will not be long but you must wait for a while yet.'

The recollection of the wider conflict came back to her. 'The war! How is it going? Have we got the Bulgars on the run?'

'Better than that. The Bulgarians sued for peace the day our forces took Skopje. The armistice has been signed.'

'Then why aren't our people in Belgrade already?'

'Because the Germans are not yet ready to admit defeat. But it cannot be long, now. New towns fall to our troops every day. The Germans are being beaten back on the Western Front, too. Everyone says they cannot sustain the fight here as well.' He laid his hand on her forehead. 'Now, no more talking. You must rest and eat and regain your strength.'

The days passed slowly. Leo slept and woke and slept again and tried to summon up the energy to eat, until one morning she woke and felt that she was ready to get up. She slid out of bed, on to legs as wobbly and uncontrolled as a newborn colt, and began to look for her clothes. At that moment Jeannie came in.

'Oh, no! No, you don't! Doctor Pierre has said you must stay in bed for at least another week.'

'Oh, don't be silly!' Leo responded. 'If I go on lying around I shall just get weaker. It'll do me good to get back to work.'

Jeannie retreated, but only to fetch Leseaux. He hurried in and took Leo firmly by the arm. 'No, no, *ma petite*. You must stay in bed. You know as well as I do that once the fever is gone there can still be complications. We are not – what is the English expression? – not out of the woods yet. You must be patient.'

By that time Leo had realized that she was not as strong as she had imagined and she was not sorry to give in and return to bed, but over the next few days her frustration increased. News of the advances made by French and Serb troops only increased her impatience. On the tenth of October news came that they had taken Pristina and the following day the town of Prizren fell. Then, at last, they heard that the Germans had asked the American President, Woodrow Wilson, to arrange an armistice with the Serbs. The whole hospital rang with cheers at the news.

That evening Leo felt the symptoms she had been dreading. Her temperature went up in a sudden peak and she began to cough and find it difficult to breathe. She had nursed enough sufferers to know what that meant. The complications mentioned by Leseaux had set in. She was suffering from bronchitis, which might easily turn into pneumonia.

For two weeks Leo fought for her life, and Leseaux and

the rest of the staff fought with her. There were times when she felt she was sinking into a bottomless well, from which she would never surface; but at those moments a vision came to her to call her back – a vision of a small, chubby-cheeked girl with amber hair. She had never seen her daughter but she was convinced that in some mysterious way the child had been sent to keep her alive and she struggled to live for her sake. And eventually the fever lost its hold on her and she began the slow process of recovery.

One morning Leseaux came into her room and after he had carried out his usual checks he said, 'Well, today is a great day. Do you know what the date is?'

'I have no idea.'

'It is November the first and today the Serbs will re-enter Belgrade. For us, the war is over.'

'Oh, praise God!' Leo exclaimed weakly. 'But how I wish I could be there to see it!'

'You are well on the way now. I think today you could get up for a while and sit in a chair. Tomorrow you can walk round the room. Soon you will be well enough to travel. But are you sure you want to go to Belgrade? You told me your child has been taken by her father's family. I do not think it will be easy to persuade them to give her up.'

'I should never forgive myself if I didn't try,' Leo said. 'At least . . . at the very least . . . I must see her. And then, if it seems she is happy and being well cared for . . .'

She faded into silence. In the last few days the thought had dogged her that Alexandra might be better off with her own people, speaking the language she had learned at her foster mother's knee and with the wealth and prestige that came with her father's rank. Even if she could persuade or force the countess to hand her over, would she be doing the child a favour? She had been roughly transplanted from one home to another already. Would it not be cruel to inflict another upheaval on her? But Leo could not forget the vision that had sustained her through her illness. She knew that she could not give up until she had at least seen the real child.

★   ★   ★

Ten days later Leo was on the train to Belgrade. Before leaving she had had to say farewell to the people she had lived and worked with for months. The field hospital was no longer needed. The patients had either been discharged or moved to other hospitals and the staff were going back to the various countries from which they had come. Pierre Leseaux was returning to Paris, to pick up the threads of his former medical practice. Saying goodbye to him had been hardest of all and Leo felt she had lost her last close friend. Sitting on the train as it rattled through the war-devastated countryside she thought that she had never been so alone. Even the prospect of returning to England held no comfort. Tom was no longer there, waiting for her. Ralph and her grandmother were both dead and she had no other family. Her mail had caught up with her just before she left Skopje but the few letters had only served to remind her of her isolation. She had never endeared herself to what was called 'society' and her only close friends before the war had been the women who trained with her in the FANY, but her decision to leave Lamarck in favour of joining Mabel Stobart in Serbia had not been popular and in the upheaval of the following months it had been hard to keep in touch with anyone. Then, when she eventually returned to England after the birth of her child she had been too depressed to make an effort to renew contacts so long left dormant. Her letters consisted of statements from her bank, a couple of reports from her estate manager at Bramwell and a long letter from Victoria, which only served to emphasize the distance between them.

To pass the time on the journey Leo took the letter out of her handbag and reread it. Victoria wrote in enthusiastic terms about the beauties of the New Zealand landscape and the warmth of the welcome she had been given by Luke's family.

Of course, she went on, *it was a bit daunting to find myself with a ready-made family, not just in-laws but children as well. But I must say they seem to have accepted me more easily than I had any right to expect. Anton is a fine lad.*

He will be six next birthday and is very independent and gallops around on his pony as if he was born in the saddle. He even sounds like a New Zealander, except that he still speaks Macedonian Serb with his grandmother. She is a magnificent old girl, and determined to keep her Macedonian heritage alive. Of course, she isn't his real grandmother. I still find it hard to remember that he is Sophie and Iannis's son and so no blood relation to Luke or anyone else here. Poor Sophie! When I think back to those far-off days at the hospital in Adrianople I remember how much in love she and Iannis were. I think she probably came to love Luke just as much, but they had so little time together before he was sent back to Europe. Just long enough for her to conceive little Nadia but not enough for him to see his baby daughter.

She's a beautiful child but likes to have her own way and creates hell when she doesn't get it. I think Luke's mother is quite relieved to hand over the reins to someone else, but I don't want to become the wicked stepmother who only wields the big stick (metaphorically, of course), so I'm trying to strike a balance between spoiling her and instilling some discipline. (Not easy.)

Family life has its complications but I find I enjoy it much more than I thought I would. Perhaps that's because of my last and best bit of news. I'm pregnant! It must have happened on the boat home because the baby is due in January. I can't get over it because I honestly thought I should never be able to have a child, after what happened. (Leo had read that sentence over several times, but without finding any explanation. She had no recollection of anything happening to her friend that might have given rise to such fears.) *So we shall be a triple-decker family!* the letter went on. *And in a wonderful way it seems to bring together all the things that have happened to us over the last six years – Bulgaria: you and me and Luke; Adrianople, with Sophie and Iannis; Luke and Sophie, then Luke and me again. There's only one thing missing. Darling, forgive me for rambling on like this. I don't know if you have managed to find Alexandra or not. I hope and pray that you have. All I need now to be completely happy is to see you with your own little girl. Please write! And if you possibly*

can, come out to stay with us. There will always be a warm
welcome for you here and I know you'd love the place.
All my love,
Victoria

Leo refolded the letter. Perhaps there was one gleam of hope
on the horizon. If she had to leave Alexandra with the Malkovic
family maybe she could sell up all her property in England
and start a new life in New Zealand.

It was dark by the time the train drew into the terminus.
Leo hailed a taxi and asked to be taken to the Hotel Moscow,
the only name she could remember. The sight of the hotel's
green and white art nouveau frontage brought back a flood of
memories. This was where Ralph had brought her when he
had dragged her back in disgrace from Adrianople; where she
had at first been incarcerated, forbidden to go out without her
grim chaperone, and then liberated to be the toast of Belgrade
society. This was where she had dressed to go to the ball
where Sasha had first seen her as a woman, and the place to
which she had returned heartbroken, a few weeks later, when
he had told her that they could never marry. Six years and a
war had passed since then and she hardly recognized the girl
she had been in those days, but checking in to the hotel gave
her an uncanny sensation that time had somehow folded back
on itself.

Her first impulse the next morning was to set out for the
Malkovics' town house and demand to see the countess, but
a look in the mirror made her change her mind. She had
brought very few clothes with her on her return to Salonika
and most of those had been left behind when she rejoined
the field hospital. For months she had worn nothing but her
nurse's dress and apron or the serviceable tweed breeches and
tunic, with or without the accompanying skirt, which had
constituted her FANY uniform. Now, looking at herself, she
saw how shabby and dirty they were. Moreover, she had lost
weight during her illness and they now hung on her as if
they had been made for a much larger woman. It was months
since she had been to a hairdresser and, though she had
refrained this time from chopping her auburn locks short,

her hair now resembled an untidy bird's nest. Her face was weather-beaten and her hands were rough and her nails broken. If she was going to present herself as a suitable person to care for any child she realized she would have to smarten herself up.

She found the dressmaker who had made clothes for her all those years ago, still in business and delighted to see her. Customers were few and far between now and the woman promised to have something ready by the next morning. Leo went to the post office and telegraphed to her bank to make arrangements for her to draw money, and then to a beauty parlour where she had her hair done and had a facial and a manicure. She bought new underwear and shoes. That done, she had time on her hands to wander round the city. It was a very different place from the lively metropolis that she remembered. Four years of enemy occupation had left the streets shabby and many of the shops shuttered, but there was a sense of optimism and excitement among the people. Only a few days before King Peter had made a ceremonial return to the city and there were still national flags in many windows and traces of the bunting that had welcomed him.

Leo's steps inevitably took her to the area where the great houses of the nobility stood. In some there were signs of occupation but many were empty, their windows shuttered and their paint peeling, their owners either killed in the war or fled to their country estates or abroad. Her heartbeat quickened as she approached the Malkovic house, but it too was closed and neglected. It was clear that if she wanted to find the family who had taken charge of her child she would have to make her way to their country estate.

Twenty

The next morning, dressed in a jade-green wool suit and feeling slightly exposed round the ankles in the new shorter skirt, she hired a car and set off for the Malkovic estate. She had only been there once, on that never-to-be-forgotten occasion of Sasha's 'Slava day' six years ago; but even if she had known the route better it would have been hard to recognize. The roads had been torn up by lorries and gun carriages and the surrounding fields were criss-crossed by trenches. Orchards which she remembered dropping blossom as they passed were now reduced to blackened stumps by shellfire. Nevertheless, after stopping two or three times to ask directions, she found herself at last driving up to the house. On her previous visit it had been decked with flags in celebration and the gardens had been full of spring flowers. Now surrounded by bare branches and drifts of autumn leaves it looked melancholy and neglected, but she was relieved to see there were definite signs of occupation. Smoke rose from the chimneys and lamplight in one window brightened the autumnal afternoon.

Leo stopped the car outside the front door and sat for a moment, breathing deeply and rehearsing in her mind what she planned to say. In her handbag she had the letter which Sasha had written just before he was killed and which she had carried with her ever since like a talisman. She knew it by heart but she took it out now and read it over to bolster her courage. *I have rewritten my will in the last few hours and had it duly witnessed. In it, I repudiate my marriage to Eudoxie on the grounds of non-consummation and declare you to be my affianced bride. If I should die here, my estate is to go to our son, or daughter.* She folded the letter and put it back in her bag. Then she got out of the car and rang the doorbell.

She had to wait so long that she almost rang again but then the door was opened by a young girl in a maid's cap and apron who regarded her with wide eyes, as if any visitor was a cause for alarm. Leo held out a visiting card.

'My name is Leonora Malham Brown. I should like to speak to the countess.'

The girl took the little square of pasteboard and scuttled off towards the back of the house, but as she did so a door opened further along the hall and a small child toddled into view pulling a toy horse on wheels and crowing with mischievous laughter. Leo froze in disbelief. This was the chubby-cheeked, auburn-haired infant of her feverish visions. The likeness was so uncanny that she feared she might be hallucinating and wondered for an instant if the sickness had returned.

'Alexandra?' She took two unsteady steps towards the child, then halted again as a man's voice spoke from the room beyond the door.

'No, Lexi, not out there. Come back.'

Leo's head swam. She had walked into a world of fantasy. First the child, now this. The voice was Sasha's.

A figure appeared in the doorway, silhouetted against the lamplight beyond.

'Lexi, come . . .' The words broke off abruptly. For an instant neither of them spoke. Then he said, 'Leonora? Is it possible?'

Her hands were at her mouth, suppressing a sound that was half-scream, half-cry of joy. 'Sasha? They told me you were dead.'

He came towards her and she was able to see his face for the first time. It was thinner and there were deep creases around his mouth, and his dark hair was liberally streaked with grey. She saw with a jolt that his left sleeve was empty and pinned to his jacket.

'Leo? I can't believe it. They said you had died when the child was born.'

'No! No! I was unconscious. They took her away because I couldn't feed her. I've been looking for her ever since. But you . . . where have you been?'

He reached out then and laid his hand on her arm and at the warmth of his touch something gave way within her and she began to weep. He swept her to him with his good arm and held her close and she burrowed her face into his shoulder and breathed in the unforgettable smell of him and knew that he was, truly, alive.

'Oh, my darling, my darling!' he whispered. 'I have been so alone! So bereft! I thought I had lost you.'

'So have I,' she gulped. 'Oh, Sasha, I can't tell you how lonely I've been.'

She felt a hand tugging her skirt and a small body tried to insert itself between her legs and his. Looking down she saw Alexandra gazing up, her thumb in her mouth, eyes wide and puzzled.

Sasha said softly, 'Darling, you know who this is, don't you?'

Leo knelt beside the child. 'Of course I know. I've seen her in my dreams for nearly two years.' She touched the delicate skin of her baby's face and a quiver of delight ran through all her nerves. 'Alexandra, darling, I've wanted to see you for such a long time. I'm so happy to have found you.'

Sasha knelt with her. 'Lexi, this is your mama. We thought we had lost her, didn't we? But here she is, after all. And now we shall all be very, very happy together.'

Leo heard footsteps and the swish of a skirt and looked up, expecting to confront Eudoxie, but it was the Dowager Countess, Sasha's mother, who held out her arms in joyful welcome.

'Leonora, my dear child! What a wonderful surprise. God is good indeed!'

Leo got up and embraced her. 'Dear Lady Malkovic! It's wonderful to see you, too. How are you?'

'Oh, I am as well as anyone of my age can expect to be. But you . . . you are so thin! You have been ill?'

'Yes, I have. But I'm better now. And . . . the Countess Eudoxie? How is she?'

Sasha's mother squeezed her hand. 'Eudoxie died a year ago, in Athens. You remember her chest was weak. When she caught the flu it was all over very quickly.'

'Oh, I'm . . .' Leo was about to make the conventional reply but closed her mouth on it. She was not sorry and they would all know it was a lie. Instead she turned to Sasha. 'But you . . . Where? How . . .?'

He put his arm round her. 'It's too long a tale to be told in a sentence. Come in and sit down by the fire.'

The countess said, 'I'll take Alexandra to the nursery and play with her. You two have so much to say to each other.' She took the child's hand. 'Come, Lexi. Let's see if cook has made any more of those nice biscuits, shall we?'

Alexandra allowed herself to be led away and Leo almost ran after her but Sasha recognized the impulse and held her back. 'There will be plenty of time later. Come and sit down.'

The countess looked over her shoulder. 'I'll tell them to send in some refreshments. I'm sure Leonora must be hungry.'

Sasha led her into a room lined with bookshelves and they sat side by side on a couch in front of a wood fire.

'Now, tell me, please!' Leo begged. 'When I saw you just now I thought I was dreaming.'

'I understand,' he replied. 'I hadn't prayed, exactly, because I thought it was pointless, but when I saw you standing there it felt like a miracle.'

'But who told you I was dead?' she asked.

'It's all part of the long story I have to tell you. Please, try not to blame me for letting you suffer for so long. Not only did I not know you were alive, I didn't know who I was myself for months.'

'What do you mean?'

'What were you told about my supposed death?'

'I heard that you had been mortally wounded in a battle near Lavci and that the fighting was so fierce they couldn't even bring your body back.'

He nodded. 'That makes sense, but I remember nothing. My first recollection is of coming round in a Bulgarian hospital and not knowing who I was or how I got there. Does that seem possible to you?'

'Perfectly possible. I've nursed enough badly wounded men to know that it can happen. But memory usually comes back in a day or two.'

'It didn't for me. But what made it worse was that I had been stripped of everything that might have identified me.'

'Stripped? How? When?'

'On the field of battle, I presume. There are always those who will grab the opportunity of scavenging for anything valuable once the fighting is over. It might have been local people, but more likely it was Bulgarian soldiers. I've never seen an army so desperately short of even basic necessities, like boots and warm clothing, as well as weapons. Anyway, it seems that a Bulgarian medical team was scouring the battlefield looking for the wounded and they came across me. I was unconscious and stripped almost naked. Even my signet ring had gone.' He glanced down at the empty sleeve. 'Whether my hand was blown off in the fighting, or someone cut it off while I was unconscious to get the ring I shall never know.'

Leo shuddered. 'That's a terrible thought!'

'Well, these things happen. If it hadn't been the depths of winter, so that the arteries froze, I should probably have bled to death. The point is, without any insignia or means of identification they had no means of knowing whether I was one of their own or an enemy. So that was how I came to be in a hospital for Bulgarian soldiers. Of course, as soon as I opened my mouth they realized I was a Serb, but to do them justice they kept me until I was strong enough to be transferred to a prisoner-of-war camp.'

'And you still couldn't remember who you were?'

'No, not with any certainty. Sometimes I got flashes of memory, like pictures from a book, but I couldn't tell if they were things that had really happened or something I'd read or been told about. And, of course, as the Bulgarians didn't know who I was or what rank I held I was sent to a camp for ordinary soldiers, not officers, so there was no one who recognized me and could tell me who I was. At least,' he paused and smiled ironically, 'there were men there who had served under me but I suppose they had only seen me at a distance and by then I looked so different – thin and ragged and unkempt – that it's not surprising they didn't know me. The first time I looked in a mirror after I got out I hardly recognized myself. All you could see was two eyes peering out of a mass of hair and beard.'

'So you did remember, in the end?'

'Slowly. The flashes of memory got stronger and clearer,

and also I kept feeling that I had a right to command. I wanted to give the other men orders. Then one morning I woke up with this name in my head – Alexander Malkovic – Colonel Malkovic. And I thought, perhaps that's who I am. But when I went to the commandant and asked to be transferred to an officers' camp he only laughed. He said I wasn't the first one to try that on and unless I could prove my identity I would have to stay where I was. He pointed out, quite reasonably, that none of the men in the camp had recognized me. So I decided he must be right. I thought perhaps I'd served under Malkovic, or heard of him some-where.' He half-closed his eyes and shook his head. 'I can't describe how terrible those months were. I kept getting these images in my mind – pictures of a childhood I thought couldn't be mine; pictures of you; memories of battles – and none of it made sense. I honestly began to believe I'd gone mad. And then I got ill again. I don't know if it was this flu that is going round or some other infection. Food was very short and we were all weak. And the fever just left me even more confused.'

'Oh, my poor love!' Leo murmured. 'But you did remember in the end. How did it happen?'

'When I got out of the prison hospital they moved me to a different POW camp. One day a man I hadn't seen before came up to me and said, "I know you. You're Colonel Malkovic, aren't you? The others don't recognize you, but I'd know you anywhere. You were my CO back in the first war when we kicked the Turks out. What are you doing in here with us lot?" He was a pretty unsavoury-looking crea-ture, but at that moment I could have embraced him. Then he said something that really stopped me in my tracks. He said, "What's it worth to you to know you've got a kid out there somewhere?" It seems he'd been listening to some of the other men gossiping and one of them had actually been in Lavci that night, the night I was supposed to have been killed, and knew that you had been there and had given birth.' He had been looking into the fire but now he turned his eyes to her. 'Leo, what on earth were you doing there, in your condition?'

'They sent word to the hospital in Bitola that you had been wounded – they said wounded, not killed. Pierre Leseaux went with an ambulance to fetch you back and I insisted on going too. He didn't want me to but I was terrified that . . .' she faltered, '. . . after that last meeting, when you were so angry, I was terrified that we might not have a chance to put things right between us. I didn't know how close I was to my time. But it was hearing the news that you had been killed that brought it on.'

He held her close. 'My poor, foolish darling. You must have had a terrible time.'

'I don't remember much about it now. In the end Pierre gave me chloroform and by the time I came round I was back in the hospital in Bitola and he'd given the baby away to that woman. I never even saw her until today.'

'How cruel! Whatever possessed him?'

'He did what he thought was best. And he was right. I probably owe him my life – and so does Alexandra.'

'It was my fault you were there at all,' he said. 'I behaved abominably to you. I knew that afterwards. I wrote you a letter. Did you ever get it?'

She reached for her bag and took out the envelope. 'You mean this one?'

'You have it with you, after all this time?'

'I have never let it go. It was all I had to hold on to. And besides, today, I thought I might need it.'

'Need it? Why?'

'I don't know how Alexandra got here, but I was told by the woman who fostered her that a man had come and taken her to be with her family. I thought Eudoxie must have somehow heard about her and decided that as your heir she should be brought up here. I thought I might need the letter to persuade her to let me take her.'

'You've been in Skopje?'

'Yes, of course. I've been looking for her for months.'

He rubbed his cheek against her hair. 'What a nightmare! I'm so sorry, my love.'

'It isn't your fault. Go on with your story.'

There was a tap on the door and the little maid came

in with a tray bearing the traditional Serbian welcome offering of jam and water, and steaming cups of sweet black coffee. Sasha took a spoonful of the jam and held it to her lips. She sucked it in and felt her nerves tingle with the unaccustomed sweetness. Food had been in short supply everywhere and even in the hotel there had been nothing to eat but bread and cabbage and gristly meat. For the first time she understood how much the jam she had collected in England and sent out to the soldiers in Bitola had meant to them. She washed the jam down with a sip of water and then a sip of coffee.

'Real coffee! Sasha, how have you managed it?'

'I can't take any credit for that. My steward had the presence of mind to wall up all our preserves and the best wine at the back of the cellar before the Bulgarians took over. They never suspected it was there.'

Leo finished the coffee and leaned back against him. 'Go on. What happened next?'

'Where was I?'

'You were talking about the man who recognized you.'

'Oh, yes. His name was Slobodan and he wasn't as stupid as he made out. He told me that the man who had been in Lavci remembered that he and others had been sent out to scour the village for a woman to be a wet nurse for the child. They assumed from that, understandably, that you must have died. The amazing thing was that the man even recalled the name of the woman – but Slobodan wouldn't tell me what it was.'

'Why not?'

'Because he wanted a reward for finding the child. Of course, I told him that when we finally got out of prison he could ask for anything he liked if he helped me find her, or him. But he didn't trust me enough at that stage to take the chance. And I didn't press him. All I could think of at that point was that you were dead. It was as if I'd found you and lost you again within a couple of minutes.'

Leo lifted her head and kissed his cheek and they were both silent for a few moments. Then she said, 'So how did you find her?'

'Slobodan promised that if we could get out he would

come to Lavci with me to find them. I'd had no incentive to escape up to that point but from that day we began to make plans. After a while we noticed that there seemed to be fewer and fewer guards. The Bulgars had decided that the war was lost and they'd heard that there were riots in Sophia. They weren't getting supplies and I think they were as hungry as we were, so they started deserting in increasing numbers. The regime got slacker and slacker and one morning Slobo and I just walked out through the gate, when one sentry went off duty and his replacement didn't show up. We started walking, aiming to go south to Lavci, but we had no money and no food and our clothes were in rags. We lived on berries and roots, but there was precious little of anything left in the fields. The locals had had whatever there was. I still wasn't strong and after a while I realized I couldn't go on without food. I suggested coming back here, but Belgrade was still in enemy hands and anyway it was too far away. It turned out that Slobo came from Skopje, which was much closer, so he suggested we went there instead. His father is a cloth merchant in a small way and the family was not well off but they treated me as if I was a second son. I was in a pretty bad way by the time we got there and they fed me and looked after me until I got my strength back. But then we had an amazing stroke of luck . . .'

'How?'

'We had to explain to the family where we were trying to get to and why and Slobo's mother mentioned that Skopje was full of refugees. In fact, she knew a family in the next street who had taken some in, so she suggested we should ask them if they knew anyone from Lavci.'

'And they did?'

'No. That would have really been a miracle. But they told us there was a café in the town where refugees sometimes met to try to find out about missing relatives. So Slobo started to hang around the place and ask questions. I was still more or less confined to bed, but I have to give him credit for persistence. It was several days before he got any help, but then he met someone who recognized the name – Popovic, wasn't it? They didn't know exactly where these people were staying but they had a rough idea of the area, so he started knocking on doors and asking if anyone knew them. I was beginning to lose hope by this point and come to the conclusion that we would have to go south to Lavci as soon as I was able to travel. Then, one evening Slobo came home and said he thought he'd found them. There was a woman with a foster child who said she came from Lavci, but she wouldn't let him take the child away unless he could prove he had been sent by the family. She showed him a gold locket which had been left with the baby and said that unless he could tell her what was inscribed inside it she wouldn't believe him.'

'The locket you gave me, all those years ago, when we thought we should never meet again,' Leo said, with a catch in her voice.

He reached inside his shirt and took out a locket on a slender gold chain. 'The very one,' he agreed. 'But I don't know how Alexandra came to have it.'

'That was Pierre's doing. I was terribly upset when I realized it was missing but he told me he had left it round the baby's neck so that if there was ever any question about her identity she would have some proof.'

'Clever man!' Sasha said. 'We owe Pierre Leseaux a great debt, one way and another. I'd like to meet him and thank him.'

'Well,' she said, 'you'll have to go to Paris to do it.'

'All in good time,' he promised.

'So she showed Slobodan the locket. Then what?'

'Of course, he had no idea what was inscribed inside it but when he told me I knew at once that it must be this one, and that the inscription was my family motto. So I wrote it out and Slobodan took it back the following day to show the woman. I don't imagine she could actually read it, but presumably she was able to match the letters with the inscription and it was enough to satisfy her, because within a couple of hours he was back, bringing Alexandra with him.'

'Oh, that must have been wonderful!' Leo said, her voice shaking. 'But how was she? She must have been frightened, being taken away from the people she knew by a stranger.'

'Yes, she must have been, but she didn't show it. She was very quiet. It was several days before I could get a word out of her. And she was thin – you wouldn't believe it to look at her now – and dirty and ridden with lice.'

'Oh, no!' Leo drew back and looked at him in dismay. 'I always imagined that whatever happened she was being looked after properly.'

'Well, bear in mind that the whole family had had to take to the road as refugees. There were older children, I understand, and it must have been hard to keep them all fed and clean. Mrs Popovic probably did the best she could, in the circumstances.'

'I didn't take to her, when I finally tracked her down,' Leo said bitterly. 'I think she was glad to get rid of Alexandra.'

'Perhaps. It was one less mouth to feed. But we shouldn't judge her too harshly. After all, Lexi was alive and she hadn't suffered any real harm. Plenty of children in those conditions wouldn't have survived. And she soon started to pick up. Slobodan's mother was wonderful. She bathed her and got rid of the lice. Her daughter had a little girl a year or two older, so she passed on some clothes for her.'

'What kind people! You did reward Slobodan, as you promised, didn't you?'

'Of course I did. He's here, working as a gardener. I offered him money but he said he would rather have a job and somewhere to live, so he would have some security. He wanted to propose to his childhood sweetheart. I settled them both in a cottage on the estate and they seem very happy. I'll take you to meet them tomorrow.'

'And Alexandra wasn't upset when he brought her to you? She didn't cry?'

'We had a few tantrums, but that came later. I think to begin with she was just overwhelmed. I imagine as the baby of the family, in difficult circumstances, she had been used to well, not neglect exactly, but having to wait for her share of whatever was going. Suddenly she was the centre of everyone's attention, made a fuss of, given all she wanted to eat. I don't think it took her long to realize that her life had taken a turn for the better. The problem now, of course, is that she expects to get her own way all the time.'

'Poor little lamb,' Leo murmured. 'She deserves a bit of spoiling.'

He leaned back and put his fingers under her chin to lift her face to his. 'So do you, my love. I've been so busy telling my story that I haven't asked about you. You told my mother you'd been ill. You look pale and thin. Are you really better?'

'Yes, I'm all right now. I had the flu, like so many other people, but I suppose I'm one of the lucky ones.'

'You said you had been looking for Alexandra for months. But how? The war has only been over for a couple of weeks.'

'I came back to Salonika at the beginning of the year. I rejoined Pierre's field hospital in the summer, just before the last big push started. We followed the Schumadia Brigade up through the Sar mountains.'

'Through the Sar? I heard about that. Miscic conducted an amazing offensive, but what a feat of endurance! And you were with them?'

'Yes, until we reached Skopje. That was where I went down with the flu.'

'You are amazing! But have you been in Macedonia all the time, from when Alexandra was born?'

'No. They sent me back to England to recuperate. I didn't want to go but I was too ill to argue. I was home for a year – the worst year of my life. I was desperate to come back but there was no point as long as the stalemate persisted on the Salonika front.'

'Did you come back alone?'

'No. Victoria was with me. Do you remember her from Adrianople?'

'Only vaguely.'

'She has been a wonderful friend to me. I don't know how I would have got through the last two years without her. But she has gone to New Zealand now. She married Luke. He was at Adrianople, too.'

'And your brother, Ralph? And Tom? I know they were both fighting on the Western Front. Are they . . .'

'Ralph was killed near a place called Passchendaele. And Tom was badly wounded. He recovered, but he was confined to a wheelchair. I heard last spring that he had died of flu, like so many others.'

'I'm sorry to hear that. I liked Tom – even if he was technically your fiancé.' He sighed deeply. 'This terrible flu! After all the thousands that have died in the war it seems as though the flu will kill thousands more. It makes you wonder if God has decided to purge the world, like another Noah's flood.'

'I don't believe God has anything to do with it,' Leo said firmly. 'Why would he purge the best and bravest? It's our own weakness and folly that's to blame.'

'For the war, perhaps. But for the flu?'

'Perhaps if we hadn't been stupid enough to go to war we would have had more strength, and more resources to fight the flu.' She shook her head and sighed in her turn. 'Anyway, here we are and it's up to us, the survivors, to see that we don't make the same mistakes again.'

He looked into her eyes. 'Us, the survivors. Yes. Now that Tom and Ralph are gone, are you completely alone in the world?'

'I was, until I found you and Alexandra.'

'And now? Are you still prepared to give up your adventurous life to settle down as the wife of a country gentleman?'

'Is that what you still intend to be?'

'If I am allowed to. Serbia is going to be very different. Different people are in charge. Who knows what may happen. But that is what I hope for.'

'And it's all I dream of, too.'

He kissed her, properly, on the lips, for the first time since they were reunited and she felt the hard knot of pain and loss at the core of her being begin to loosen.

The door opened and small feet pattered across the room. A voice demanded: 'Up, Papa! Up!'

Sasha reached down and lifted the child on to his knee. She clung round his neck and, with her free hand, tried to remove Leo's from his shoulder.

'My papa! Mine!'

'I know, darling,' Leo said. 'But I love him, too. I love you both. I never meant to leave you but it wasn't my fault. And I'll never leave you again. I promise.'

'Your mama has had a long journey and she's been ill, so she needs us to look after her just like Grandmama and I look after you,' Sasha said gently. 'Will you help us?'

The child regarded Leo with solemn, unblinking eyes for a moment. Then she nodded and Sasha carefully lifted her on to Leo's lap. For the first time Leo cradled her to her breast and felt the warm, silken skin of her face against her neck. Sasha reached across and slipped the chain of the locket over her head. She pressed the clasp and it opened to display a twist of black hair.

'You told me when you gave it to me that one day I should take out your hair and replace it with a lock of my firstborn child's.'

'It didn't seem possible, then, that it might be our child.'

Very gently, she ran her hand over the baby's head. A few delicate hairs came away in her fingers. She opened the compartment in the locket and carefully wound the dark hair and the auburn together and replaced them in the locket. She raised her eyes to Sasha's.

'Survivors,' she said. 'You once said that if we could be together we could face the whole world. Now there are three of us and we can build a new world, better than the old one.'